NANCY PARKER'S

Spooky Speculations

MAIDSERVANTS, MYSTERY AND MURDER!

OXFORD
UNIVERSITY PRESS

Great Clarendon Street, Oxford OX2 6DP
Oxford University Press is a department of the University of Oxford.
It furthers the University's objective of excellence in research, scholarship,
and education by publishing worldwide. Oxford is a registered trade mark
of Oxford University Press in the UK and in certain other countries

British Library Cataloguing in Publication Data

Data available

ISBN: 978-0-19-274697-9

1 3 5 7 9 10 8 6 4 2

Printed in Great Britain

Paper used in the production of this book is a natural,
recyclable product made from wood grown in sustainable forests.
The manufacturing process conforms to the environmental
regulations of the country of origin.

NANCY PARKER'S

Spooky Speculations

by

JULIA LEE

ILLUSTRATED BY CHLOE BONFIELD

OXFORD
UNIVERSITY PRESS

NULLIUS IN VERBA

— motto of the Royal Society

Meaning 'Take nobody's word for it', an expression of the resolve of the Fellows of the Royal Society to withstand the domination of authority and to verify all statements by an appeal to facts determined by experiment.

www.royalsociety.org

1. A NEW CHAPTER

NANCY'S JOURNAL

I am writing this on the train on my way to begin a New Chapter in my life! That accounts for the slitely wobbly handWriting.

Since my last job as a housemaid ended I have been working on Ethel Boyd's dad's Fruit & Veg stall. Working on a market stall is <u>not</u> a job worth writing a diary about. Every day the same—selling muddy spuds & spotty apples & putting up with customers complaining.

But then the letter came. The letter which RESCUED ME from misery! I will glue it in here.

High Gables, The Green, Seabourne, Sussex.

29th September 1920

Dear Nancy,

Sorry for not writing sooner. I have been
extraordinarily busy with my hateful new school,
and homework, and lines. Lines are a punishment
they dish out just for saying things like the title
of the composition set by Miss Eagle, our English
teacher, was not very original. 'What I Did In The
Holidays'! The older girls say she sets it every
year. Of course, I wrote a thrilling account of our
adventures solving a mystery together. But Miss
Eagle called it 'highly fanciful' and said we were
not asked to make up fairy tales, then gave me yet
more lines when I said I could show her the newspaper
clippings to prove it. What it is to be among fools . . .!

The reason I am writing is because I have some good
news. Do you remember Miss Dearing? The old
lady who lives across The Green in Apple Cottage,
and drives that donkey cart? The news is that her
godfather has died and left his house to her, so she's
going to move in and is looking for a General
Servant to help her run it. Having lived alone and
looked after herself perfectly well for years, she says
she isn't used to ordering anyone about and doesn't

really like the idea of it. Nor does she want anyone who would order her about, either. So I reminded her about you.

I am sure you would not order anyone about, would you, Nancy? But I wonder if you are still working as a maidservant or if you have got some other exciting new career by now? (I expect you have!)

Miss Dearing says she will pay a 'modest but not ungenerous wage', with one day off every week, and provide the uniform. The house is called Oxcoombe Grange. It's the grandest place in Oxcoombe, a small village about five miles from here and right by the sea. Write to her straight away if you think you would like it. I'm sure you are busy doing something much more fascinating, though.

Sincerely yours,

E. Otter

P.S. I wonder what Miss Dearing's idea of a suitable uniform is? Remember, she is quite eccentric. But whatever she comes up with, it will be nothing like as bad as what I have to wear to school. Utterly gruesome!

So I did write—then Miss Dearing wrote back—& now I am off to work for her in the grandest house in the village!! Miss Dearing sent my ticket & instrucktions to change at Seabourne to the little train that goes along the coast. She will meet me at the station. Grandma has packed me up some sandwiches (fish paste) & Dad gave me a bag of biscuits from the Factory where he works— the ones that didn't come out right. I've got Custard Creams with no cream in them & Cinnamon Squares that aren't square. I don't care. They taste just as good. I like Cinnamon Squares—more like Cinnamon <u>Blobs</u>—the best.

Added to that Aunty Bee sent me off with a parcel of books. Grandma calls them PENNY DREADFULS but they cost sixpence or even a shilling. Not that Aunty Bee pays for them. She's a bus conductress & she gets them from the Lost Property Office at the bus depot. If they are still there after 3 months—and who would go back for a dog-eared old book with a torn cover? —she can take her pick. The ones we like best are <u>crime stories</u> with Detectives in & BLOOD & GORE all over the covers. But the only books Aunty Bee managed to get are a Romance (swoony lady on the cover) a Cowboy (rearing horse & clouds of dust) & a Ghost Story (big black castle on a mountain crag).

I don't care for romance or cowboys much so I have started on that one.

I am hoping Miss Dearing will be an Excellent Employer. Not like my last one. I just have 1 or 2 small doubts. (I know how to spell a hard word like DOUBT cos there was a sign on our classroom wall: 'If in doubt, ask Teacher.' But if you did you got shouted at. So that was no good, except for learning how to spell it.)

My doubts—now that I am on my way, & Miss Dearing has paid for my train ticket—turn out to be:-

1. I haven't got that much experiense in service—just 3 months in fact. I know what Housemaids <u>do</u> but I cannot really cook.

2. If it's the grandest house in the village & there's only me that will mean a LOT of WORK.

3. Just how ECCENTRIC is Miss Dearing?? (Ella is quite eccentric herself.)

4. Lastly—how small is Oxcoombe? (I am a <u>city girl</u> at heart.)

'Look on the bright side, Nancy!' —that's what Aunty Bee would say. Grandma would say 'You made your bed my girl. Now you must lie in it.' Poor Gran never looks on the bright side. (Dad never says much at all. He's been like that ever since he came back from the War.)

But I've always been a quick learner so I expect I'll cope—specially if Miss Dearing doesn't like to boss anyone about. I must put my Doubts to one side and get on with it. The main thing is that I shall be at the seaside (even if winter is coming) & I shall see Ella Otter again.

LATER

Just changed trains at Seabourne—I had to ask the Gard if this was the right one. When I said I was going to Oxcoombe Grange he pulled a funny old face. I couldn't tell if it was what I said or cos those fish paste sandwiches have left a bit of a pong behind (even tho I ate them ages ago & threw away the paper they were wrapped in!).

Pongy faces!

Then he looked at the cover of my book & said 'I see you like <u>eerie old places</u>—Oxcoombe Grange will suit you down to the ground. Two stops & you'll be there.' He was getting ready to blow his whistle so I couldn't ask more.

Not in the mood to read 'Dark Deeds At Crag Castle' any more. The train down from London was crowded but this one is empty. Leastways the sun is still shining & I hope to catch <u>my 1st glimpse of the sea</u> any moment now.

Except we're going into a tunnel—

A long tunnel—

And now we've come out into THICK FOG.

2. THE WORD OF THE DAY

Ella Otter jumped down from the train at the tiny station of Seabourne Halt. The platform was completely empty. She tore off her maroon felt hat—or *porridge pot* as it was known in school slang—and flung it to the ground as the train steamed away. She was small and square and her school blazer was a bit too big. Her bobbed black hair was hat-shaped now.

'School is stinky!' she yelled.

Every afternoon Ella thought up a single word to describe her school day. Yesterday it had been 'Dull'; the day before, 'Dire'. Today it was 'Stinky,' and she chanted it out loud as she trudged up the lane from the station. If anyone challenged her—not that there was a single soul about—she would put on an innocent face and say, 'But school *was* stinky today.' Something had gone wrong with a chemistry experiment and the whole class had to rush outside into the quad, gasping like goldfish, in search of fresh air.

School wasn't usually as exciting as that, just a vile mix of torment and drudgery. It was all pointless rules she never knew existed until she had broken them, and silly slang that made her feel left out. For a start, the first years were called Third Formers: the next year was Lower Fourth, then Upper Fourth, and so on, for no good reason that Ella could see, except that's how it was done. The other girls had big sisters or cousins to learn from, or were part of a group of friends who just seemed to know. Ella had always been taught at home and simply wasn't used to spending her whole day shut up in a class of twenty-five girls, in an enormous school filled with stern-looking teachers. She looked back on those days before school began as a carefree, sunlit paradise.

On the first day of term the class was made to copy their timetable into brand-new exercise books. Ella drew it out neatly, a column for each day, with blocks inside for every lesson. And then she sat back and stared at it, her mind completely boggled. Every lesson, for every day, for every week, for the whole year! What if the sun was shining and she needed to go on an adventure? What if she just felt like curling up in an armchair and reading? A timetable left no scope for that, as far as she could see.

Ella began to suspect that school was not for her.

She spoke to her father. Professor Otter was a fair-minded man. While she put her case he made a tent of his fingers and looked at her over the top. His dark brown eyes were kind. He replied in a most reasonable voice. But what he said was, 'You must give it time, Ella. Give it time. See what you think at the end of the term. You might be surprised.'

That was not the right answer.

Now she kicked her hat ahead of her up the lane. It was against school rules—not the kicking; she was sure The Authorities hadn't imagined as far as that—but being out and about in uniform without your hat was a crime, punishable by detention. Teachers were always on the lookout for misdemeanours. Prefects were even worse. They seemed to positively enjoy pouncing on girls both inside and outside school and telling them exactly what stupid, pointless rule they were breaking.

No one would spot her here, though. Seabourne Halt was in the middle of nowhere, and The Green, where she lived, was the furthest from school that you could get and still be in Seabourne. There were no other children in the houses around The Green; it was all old majors, and retired doctors, and dogs. There was only one girl from school who lived anywhere near and that was Juniper Vale. Ella only knew her name because so many of the Third Form were in awe of her and talked about her all the time.

Juniper Vale was two years ahead of Ella, in the Upper Fourth. She had golden curls, a fashionably drawling way of speaking, and captained the junior hockey team to constant victories. To Ella these were all excellent reasons for hating her. In addition, Juniper's mother was in the habit of driving too fast in her new red Daimler, with little care for anyone else using the roads.

Ella screwed up her face. She didn't want to waste another second thinking about school or anyone to do with it. Instead she turned her mind to happier things, and one of those was her friend Nancy Parker. They met when Nancy had come to work in the house next door. Girls of Ella's class were not meant to be friends with housemaids, but then Ella had never behaved as she was expected to. The girls she was supposed to make friends with were so dull and conventional—and often showed signs of not being terribly bright! But she and Nancy had much in common: both were keen observers of human nature and loved nothing better than finding a mystery to solve. Ella was very pleased that she had managed to match up Nancy with Miss Dearing. Soon she would be back!

Lost in thought, Ella turned out of the narrow lane from the station into the wider one which led towards The Green. A car came whooshing round the bend. Ella fell back, flattening herself into the hedge. The car swept past without slowing. It was dark red, huge, and shiny. And out of the rear window a face peered back at her: a disapproving face. Juniper Vale.

3. OXCOOMBE GRANGE

NANCY'S JOURNAL

I suppose <u>all</u> old houses look creepy in the fog.

Specially when the path is lined with trees all pointing their spiky fingers at you. Just like this:

And when you can't see anything much beyond cos of THICK WHITE MIST—then shapes and sounds come at you all of a sudden out of the gloom.

Miss Dearing declared it was 'Just a little SEA FOG that's drifted in. They go as quick as they come.' (Oh no it didn't.)

As promissed Miss Dearing had met me at Oxcoombe station—in a cart pulled by a donkey name of Pancho. I must say a Donkey Cart is not a very dignifyed mode of travel. Specially when it is painted <u>screaming Red & Yellow</u> like a fairground ride! Glad there was nobody else around to see us. I had forgotten quite how ORIGINAL Miss Dearing is in her dress. She doesn't wear the usual Old Unmarried Lady Outfits of dusty black coats & shapeless hats & wrinkled grey stockings.

PANCHO

MISS DEARING

Her head was bound in a purple turban fixed with a glittery pin & over her shoulders she had a cloak like a check horse blanket. Maybe it <u>was</u> a horse blanket. Her stockings were pale pink. (Aunty Bee would like those. Tho she wouldn't be seen dead in the rest!)

Miss Dearing seemed v. cheerful dispite the fog & we clattered off down the lane. I could scarce see anything past Pancho's ears & had no idea where we were going or how far we had gone. Even donkey hooves sound echo-y & spooky in such an atmos-fear.

All of a sudden tall iron gates reared up in front of us. A hunched little person all in black—like something out of a fairy tale—scuttled out from nowhere to open them & stood back watching us go in. 'Good day, Mrs Shanto!' Miss Dearing called out just as if it <u>was</u> a good day. Then she added 'By the way this is Miss Nancy Parker. Miss Parker is my housekeeper.'

Oh Lord! I thoght—so I am Housekeeper now!! (I don't look anything like one being much too young: tall & skinny with gingery hair that WILL NOT BEHAVE. Plus one or two spots which Aunty Bee says is 'my age'.) But Housekeeper sounds <u>much better</u> than General Maid.

Mrs Shanto just squinted at me like she could tell what I was thinking.

As we drove on Miss Dearing said in a low voice 'Mrs Shanto is a funny old thing—lives just across from the gates. She used to keep an eye on the Grange when my godfather was away. He was a great traveller—as you

shall find out.'

Then we came to Oxcoombe Grange itself. Or as much as I could see of it in the fog. It's <u>BIG</u>. You could fit the whole of our house at Bread Street thru the front door! Miss Dearing turned a huge iron key in the lock & then we were inside. Very cold & dark it was too! I could not help a <u>small shiver</u> & hoped my new employer didn't see it. Ahead was a long hallway with all the doors shut. I opened 1 or 2 and peeped inside. Great gloomy rooms with the blinds drawn down & the furniture shrouded all over in dust-sheets so that you couldn't tell what was underneath. I shut those doors v. quickly.

Miss Dearing was keen to tell me all about the house. The front half is the NEW PART: not much more than a hundred years old! Doesn't sound very <u>new</u> to me. We made our way towards the OLD PART—now the kitchens & so on—which dates from the days of King Henry 8th. (The one with all the wives.) 'It was my godfather who put in the electric light' she added proudly—but quite frankly the lamps were so far apart & so dim that they didn't do much to PEERCE THE GLOOM.

At the end of the hallway there was a wide staircase with carved wooden banisters—I could just picture olden-times ladies swishing down it in their great heavy skirts! Tried not to think how much sweeping & polishing those stairs would take & how much sweeping & polishing they've had over the years from long-forgotten maidservants.

As I peered up at the landing

I SAW A MAN !!

He looked very Sinister—half hidden in the shadows—just stood there glaring down at us as if we were the intruders. I shreeked so loud I heard my voice echo thru the house!!! I found I'd clutched Miss Dearing's arm hard (which is not how you should behave to an employer).

But she just laughed. Really & truly laughed—saying 'It's only a Suit of Armour.' He didn't look like any suit of armour I ever saw. (Tho I've only seen one once when Aunty Bee & me went on to trip to the Tower of London.) 'But he's got a mustache!' I said.

She told me 'That's just horsehair. It's part of the helmet—to make him look fearce.'

I felt such a fool. It's not like me to be scared so easy. I like to think I am made of sterner stuff. But everything about today—the fog & the shrouded rooms & odd little Mrs Shanto like a fairy tale goblin—not to menshun reading a Ghost Story & what that gard on the train said—everything has SET MY NERVES ON EDGE.

Turns out what looked like a man lurking on the landing is an extreemly Rare & Valuable suit of armour from an old Japanese Worrier.

I shall try and draw him here

Miss Dearing said her godfather (name of Dominic Duggan) went all over the world: mountains & deserts & jungles & ~~aynt~~ ainshunt cities. He collected stuff from every place he visited—whatever took his fancy—& had them shipped back home. 'Wherever you look about this house you will find something strange.'

To prove it she pointed upwards. Rows of stuffed animal heads hung along the wall staring down at us out of mad glass eyes. Not just any old animals like you see round here—creatures from far-away parts of the globe, with stripes & spots & curlicue horns. I felt quite sorry for them. Then I remembered who would have to climb up & dust em!!

Next Miss Dearing showed me the kitchen saying 'This is where you are in charge!' She asked me if I could get the cooking range going to warm the place up & boil water for some tea. She asked in such a <u>nice tone</u> with such a <u>kind</u> <u>smile</u> on her face. (Just like Ella wrote—Miss D. is not happy about giving actual orders.)

I TRIED. But you never saw anything so ~~cumpil~~ cumplicated in your life! There's ovens with big doors & ovens with little doors, some for cooking & some for coal. Hotplates with such heavy lids that if one fell down it would squash your hand flat as a slice of bacon. It even has its own name:

Excelsior

Miss Dearing's gone outside to look for someone called Peg. It's cold as a church in here. I could really do with a hot cup of tea & so will Miss D. when she comes in. This is my <u>1st task as a Housekeeper</u> & I've failed it!!

I did however explore the warren of rooms here at the back (still feeling a bit funny about the house & being on my own). I found a very fat but tatty old book tucked away at the end of a high shelf. It's called

'Wise Advice from A Lady: A Guide to Strict & Sensible Household Management'.

Inside it says it's by someone called Lady Pouncey. I am not sure what A LADY knows about such stuff except for spouting orders & running her finger along a ledge to check for signs of dust! But I'm going to keep it to look at later. (Need all the tips I can get!!)

Also discovered the Coal Hole so I filled the coal bucket & set it beside the Excelsior to show I did as much as I was able. Now I'm just waiting for Miss Dearing. Decided to get out my Journal & write down everything that's happ

I just heard a BUMP.

It was <u>not</u> outside.

There's nobody in the house but me.

It's all still now & VERY SILENT.

As if something was listening—and biding its time.

4. 'YOU'VE GOT TO EXPECT NOISES'

NANCY'S JOURNAL

Never found out what made that bump.

I had to tuck this Journal away quick cos Miss Dearing came back in together with an old man & a girl. They made such a row stamping their feet & blowing on their cold hands there was no chance to hear if there were MORE NOISES.

Miss D. introduced everyone:—

* The Gardener <u>Mr Joshua Oakapple</u>. He looks like he's out of a fairy tale (Mrs Shanto's not the only one!) being wrinkle-faced & bandy-legged & you might say WISE or you might say GRUMPY. Can't tell which yet.

* The girl is <u>Peg</u>. Big & strong with fair hair & v. red cheeks as if she'd been out in the cold for ages. I know you shouldn't JUDGE PEOPLE BY THEIR APPEARANCE & heaven knows I had some peculiar clothes when I was younger (Gran used to cut down stuff of Aunty Bee's and <u>make</u> me wear it)—but Peg had on a man's jumper full of holes, heavy rubber boots & a skirt that surely started life as a curtain!

I know that people do not have to be Poor or Neglected to dress scruffy—some just choose to look that way. Ella Otter for ecksample. But I don't think Peg chose.

Once I'd said How-de-do I asked if they heard that great loud bump & they all said 'What?' which meant they hadn't. So I had to explain. I wish I did not blush so easy.

Mr Oakapple's gruff opinion was 'You've got to expect noises in an old house like this. Boards snapping, floors creaking. Stands to reason.' Miss Dearing nodded in agreement. Peg didn't say a word.

I dare say they are right. I was never in such a <u>big old house</u> as this before—there must be all sorts I don't know.

Next I had to confess I'd had no luck lighting the range. I felt even more of A FOOL by then. Peg was keen to have a go at it. She didn't say so—just got down on the floor and stuck her head inside an oven door. She waved matches & turned nobs. I don't know what she did that I hadn't tried—apart from lots of clanging & banging & bringing out a birds-nest from somewhere & making Clouds of Soot—but in the end she got it working!

The Excelsior began to throw out a nice bit of heat so once I swept up the soot I filled the kettle. Soon we were sitting round the table drinking our tea & feeling much more cheerful (<u>me</u> anyhow). (Mr Oakapple still looked grumpy.) That's when Miss Dearing began discribing her

GRAND PLAN for Oxcoombe Grange: to set up a Donkey ~~Sang~~ Sankcherry in the gardens! She means to rescue every worn-out overworked miss-treated donkey in the county. Peg's job is to look after them while I look after the house.

Miss D. <u>didn't say a thing</u> about DONKEYS in her letter. It wouldn't be the 1st time an employer has taken me on Under False Pretences. They say something like 'it is just a small quiet household' & it turns out to be quite the opposite. And you must put up with it & hold your ~~tonge~~ tongue if you want to keep your job.

I glanced round at everybody's faces—Miss Dearing excited about her plan—Peg a bit soot-smudged yet happy. But Mr Oakapple looked like he'd swallowed a frog. I could see he wasn't thrilled about the donkeys.

Not one little bit.

5. A BIT LIKE NOAH'S ARK

NANCY'S JOURNAL

After the tea Miss Dearing fetched Pancho (who was busy eating the front lawn) & we drove back to her old house at The Green: Apple Cottage. Which is where I am now. She said she had to get back FOR THE ANIMALS.

It's a bit like <u>Noah's Ark</u>. They have taken over all the garden—except for the Vegetable Patch—which as a result is v. muddy. There are:—

* geese

* hens

* ducks

* a nanny-goat
  on a long rope

* Pancho
  (brown with a fawn nose)

* another donkey called Gilda
  (grey & small &
  pretty—for a donkey)

Miss D. says her geese are as good as GARD DOGS. They did indeed seem very fearce—sticking their necks out & hissing at me for no reason at all. She also said a Goat will eat anything it can find. Anything. Even clothes off the washing line.

I find I am not nearly as fond of animals as Miss Dearing is.

After we got in from tucking the animals up for the night she heated a supper of stew made out of carrots & turnips & leeks—with dumplings. (I think she's forgotten that I am meant to be waiting on her.) She peered into the pot & told me 'I dare say you are expert at Roast Beef and pork chops and Chicken-alla-Something but we DO NOT EAT ANY MEAT in this house. We do not kill God's creatures for our food.'

Which is a great pity cos the <u>only</u> cooking I know at all is how to fry up sausages & bacon.

But then she went on 'So I shall teach you to cook VEDGETARIAN meals.' I must admit this was a great releef.

I am writing this upstairs after supper. There are only 2 bedrooms & the one Miss Dearing has put me in is very nice. Hardly a maid's room. It is papered with blue daisies—even all over the ceiling—which Miss D. says is to stop cracked bits of plaster falling on our heads. (It is a very OLD cottage.) So here I am sitting up in bed with a hot-water-bottle at my feet. Once the sun goes down it's colder in the country than in town. It's also <u>very black</u> outside the window.

My doubts have changed since this morning.
<u>Now they are:—</u>

1. Can I learn to cook VEDGETARIAN Food?

2. All those animals. (I can smell them from here.)

3. Is Oxcoombe Grange really spooky—or is it just me?

This job sounded so good when Ella first discribed it. Plus Miss Dearing is a very kind & understanding lady. Is this place worth keeping, I wunder? Well—either it's creepy Oxcoombe—or back to the Fruit & Veg stall for me!

32

6. IN A SCIENTIFIC WAY

Ella poked her head around the door of Apple Cottage and found Nancy in the kitchen, clearing the breakfast things.

'Hello. Miss Dearing said I'd find you here. You've grown!'

Nancy patted the top of her frizzy hair to flatten it. 'Hope not. You haven't changed at all,' she laughed.

'I've got new specs. Father insisted I had them for school.' Ella's glasses had tortoiseshell rims and were not—yet—mended with a twist of wire or a lump of putty. 'I can't stay long or I'll be late, and if you're late, even by a minute, you get an order mark.'

'How is school? Any better?' Nancy asked.

Ella sighed. 'The girls are silly, the teachers tedious, and the work is much too easy. As for school food—vile! Cottage pie tastes the same as apple pie, and they both taste of dishrags.'

She made a grab for the last piece of toast just as Nancy whisked the toast-rack away, and buttered it quickly before Nancy could take the butter dish, too. 'Any marmalade? No? Never mind. Now, I want to hear everything about Oxcoombe Grange!'

Nancy glanced out of the window to make sure that Miss Dearing was still busy in the garden. 'You never said it was a spooky old Museum, full of strange heads and bodies—'

'I've never actually been inside,' Ella replied. She leaned forward, eyes gleaming. 'What d'you mean, heads and bodies?!'

'There's loads of grand gloomy rooms, stuffed with things that Mr Duggan collected. Masks and stuffed animal heads that stare at you. Funny old statues and suits of armour with peculiar expressions. It's easy to mistake them for *people*.'

Nancy began washing the breakfast dishes. Ella, munching toast, just watched.

'Then there's noises,' Nancy continued.

'Noises?'

'Only one noise, really. But it gave me the creeps. Nobody else heard anything.'

'What kind of noise?'

'Sort of a bump. Like someone dropping something, or bumping into something, when there was no one else in the house but me—and I didn't make it. Mr Oakapple—he's the gardener, been there years—puts it all down to old floorboards and suchlike.'

Ella shrugged. 'Probably right.'

'You weren't there.' Nancy went a bit pink in the face. 'I've begun a new journal and I—I did mention the strange noise in it.'

Ella remembered how Nancy made notes and wrote down all her theories while they were trying to solve last summer's mystery. It proved very useful. She said, 'I'd expect nothing less. Can I see?'

'It's packed away with everything ready to go over to Oxcoombe.'

Ella glanced around. There seemed to be a great many of Miss Dearing's belongings still left, cluttered about the room, everything colourful, busy, and cheery. Very much like Miss Dearing herself.

'It doesn't look as if you've packed at all.'

'Miss Dearing's only taking what she calls *the essentials*, and most of that's to do with the animals!'

With one finger Ella drew in the toast crumbs she had scattered about the tabletop. 'Are you worried that the Grange is haunted?' she asked.

Nancy flinched. Plates clanged together in the sink. 'What makes you say that? Have you heard any stories?'

'Miss Dearing never mentioned it. She'd hardly be keen to move into a haunted house, would she? And she does seem very keen.'

'She's going to turn the grounds into a Donkey Sanctuary, that's why! You never mentioned *that*, neither.'

Ella lifted her hands as Nancy wiped away the toast crumbs with a damp cloth. It didn't occur to her to help. 'Miss Dearing said nothing to me about it, either. But it doesn't surprise me in the least. This house and garden have always been a sanctuary for lost and injured creatures. Now she'll have more land, and presumably more money, to devote to the cause.'

She watched her friend move about the kitchen, saying nothing, lips pursed.

'Nancy—you may find Oxcoombe Grange creepy at first but I'm sure there's a rational explanation. We just have to establish what it is.' She grinned. 'Yes! We should do it in a scientific way.'

Nancy stood still, the cleaning cloth dangling from her hand. 'What's that mean?'

'That means investigating anything that worries you—unexplained noises and so on—in a rigorous and methodical way. I'll come and help.'

The frown on Nancy's face cleared. 'You'd do that?'

'Try and stop me!' cried Ella. 'It will be fun. And I really need some fun, after the perdition of school every day.'

'What will Miss Dearing think? After all, it's her house.'

'We won't tell her why I'm there. I'll visit as soon as I can. What d'you say?'

In answer, Nancy grinned back at her.

'When do you go there?'

'Today, this morning, soon as the animals are ready.' Nancy peered out of the window again. 'A van is coming for the luggage, and a farm truck's taking the geese, the ducks and hens. Oh, and the goat. And then Miss Dearing's going to drive the cart with Pancho pulling it and Gilda walking behind. We'll be quite a parade. All that's missing is a big bass drum like in the Sally Army,

and a load of little kids running alongside waving flags.'
She sounded much more cheerful now.

'Oxcoombe's such a sleepy place. That should give
them something to look at. I wish I could wave you off—
but, crikey!' Ella cried, wiping butter off her mouth and
transferring buttery crumbs to her sleeve. 'Look at the
time! I must fly, or it's a late mark for me.'

7. SOMETHING WRONG

Ella's teacher, Miss Canning, had just finished taking the register when a prefect came tapping at the form-room door. She murmured something to Miss Canning, who then glanced about the class with *that expression* on her face; the expression that said she could see right inside everyone's heads. Ella resented the feeling that anyone could know the contents of her brain—and then she worried that Miss Canning could see her resentment too!

'Eleanor Otter,' Miss Canning said in her clipped voice. 'Miss Chard wishes to see you.'

Miss Chard. There was a definite—but hushed—intake of breath all round the room. Miss Chard was the Deputy Head. Miss Chard was in charge of Discipline. And Miss Chard wanted to speak to Ella Otter.

Ella walked to the front of the classroom, feeling everyone's eyes on her back, and followed the prefect outside. The empty corridor looked extremely long. The classrooms on either side were extremely quiet. Ella's footsteps sounded extremely loud. She didn't walk beside the prefect—Third Formers simply didn't—but followed behind her, concentrating on the thick plait of dark hair that fell down her back, tied at the tail with a neat maroon ribbon.

As they came to the end of the corridor and turned the corner, she cleared her throat and said, 'D'you happen to know why Miss Chard wants to see me?'

The prefect glanced back. She gave a sympathetic smile. (Perhaps they weren't *all* so bad.) But then she said, 'You must have done something wrong, mustn't you?'

Which was exactly what Ella suspected.

The first thing she saw in Miss Chard's study was a stuffed owl which glared at her out of fierce glass eyes. Ella remembered that the ancient Greek goddess of wisdom was Athena and her symbol was an owl. Perhaps Miss Chard wanted to remind everyone in the school that girls and women were wise. Or perhaps she wanted to remind them that an owl has a sharp beak and sharp claws, and astonishingly sharp eyes that can spot a tiny field mouse crouching in the grass from miles away. Just as Miss Chard had astonishingly sharp eyes and could spot a tiny Third Former from miles away—and tell immediately if she was breaking school rules.

Ella was sure she had been summoned to see the Deputy Head because she had broken a rule. But if she had, it was bound to be something silly that she didn't even know about. That didn't prevent her from feeling apprehensive. Miss Chard was known throughout the school as a Holy Terror.

For a Holy Terror, up close Miss Chard was surprisingly small. She had iron-grey hair and tortoiseshell-rimmed spectacles which rested halfway down her nose. She glared at Ella over the spectacles.

'You're a new girl, aren't you, Eleanor?' She said the words new girl as someone else might say *smelly boot* or *warty toad*.

'Yes, Miss Chard.' Of course she was a new girl: her serge school tunic was as stiff as a board, and she hadn't quite mastered tying a tie properly, especially after Games when everyone had to hurry.

'I trust you are fully acquainted with the school rules?'

This time Ella paused before replying. If she said no it looked bad, but if she said yes it might look as if she was deliberately breaking them. Yet she couldn't think of any transgression. She hadn't run in the corridors, or even walked down the wrong side. She certainly hadn't walked on the Prefects' Lawn, or shouted at break, or been late for Assembly—or late for anything at all, not even school this morning. Her homework was immaculate and always in on time. She couldn't think of a single thing she might have done wrong, so it truly must be something so minute, so mysterious, so unheard-of, that any new girl might have made the same mistake. In the end she just gave Miss Chard a sickly, squinty sort of smile and didn't answer at all.

'Then why, Eleanor Otter, have you let the school down?' Miss Chard thundered. 'You have been seen without a hat!'

Oh, thought Ella. Of course. The hat. The hateful

porridge pot. She couldn't see why one small girl—an insignificant Third Former—without a hat was letting the whole school down. It was hardly keeping her brains in place. And she usually did wear her hat, on the train, on the walk from the station to the school grounds, right up until the moment she reached the junior cloakroom and her own peg. The only time she took the wretched thing off was when she was safely miles away, near home.

But of course a sharp-eyed owl could see for miles.

Or someone had told on her. Suddenly she knew just who: that face, framed by blonde curls, staring out of the back of a Daimler. Juniper Vale. She was very surprised that Juniper even knew who she was—a new girl, a lowly Third Former, with no older sisters or cousins already in school. But why would someone like Juniper want to tell tales on her? Why would a popular girl like Juniper need to tell tales at all?

'I am not going to give you lines, Eleanor. I understand that your English teacher has already had to set you lines, once for disobedience, and once for impertinence. This is hardly a good start. Is it, child?'

Ella tried her best to look ashamed.

'Instead I am going to set you an essay, and you will have to stay behind after school to write it. Two full pages on The Importance of Rules. Now you may go.'

Ella hurried back to her form-room, to find that everyone else had packed up and left for a geography lesson. 'Curse you, Juniper Vale!' she thought. She had already decided the word for the day: school is unjust.

44 Bread Street, London S.E.

Dear Nancy,

As the weather has turned quite sharp I am sending the good thick socks & vest I knitted you. I can't think how you left them out when you were packing. I trust this parcel reaches you safe & sound.

Your Dad's back is bad again. I make him wear a bandage soaked in Coyne's Tar Oil Liniment under his vest at night but he won't wear it to the Factory. Says it will make the biscuits come out tasting of tar.

Ethel Boyd is poorly again. That was a good job you let go on the fruit stall. Instead you have to go prancing off to the seaside as if it was the summer holidays.

Me & your Aunty Beatrice are as well as expected for the time of year. Take care of yourself & wrap up warm.

Grandma

8. A FUNNY LOT

NANCY'S JOURNAL

Oxcoombe Grange looks much less spooky without the fog.
But those narled old trees don't exackly welcome you. It
was ~~beat~~ beutiful & sunny so we could see the sea today.
There's no Promenade here—or Pier—just a bay with 2 or
3 boats bobbing about & a little stream running into it
& big cliffs on either side. Certainly a much nicer view
than any around Bread Street—which is all brick walls
& smoking chimneys. And ever so quiet! (Apart from the
chickens & geese.) I have <u>never been</u> anywhere so quiet. I
dare say I shall get used to it.

<u>My jobs today</u> (which—hurrah!—I could do):—
—get Miss Dearing's bedroom ready
—pick my own room (I chose the one right above the
   kitchen) & get that ready too.

   Miss Dearing's room is at the front of the house with
Chinese wallpaper & a sea view. The house is so big it's a
very long way away from everything else—the stairs—and
the kitchen—and ME. Took me ages going up & down with
brooms & bed linen & coal & water. The bed is what they
call a <u>4-Poster</u>. I would not care for one like it myself.

There's curtains all round it & when you close them you can't see out. Something horrible could be in the room beyond & you would never know till it was too late. (I can't help thinking of that old Japanese Worrier looking like a Burglar or some such.) If something was coming for me I should like to know beforehand & have Time To Act—even if it was only to <u>scream</u>!

Another thing. It's probbly just nerves—but when I was upstairs I did sort of keep seeing things from the corner of my eye. Flickers of shapes just out of sight. When I looked there was NOTHING THERE. I am telling myself it was NOTHING too.

By the time I'd done Miss Dearing's room I was barking like the noisiest Gard Dog due to all the dust. So I came back to the kitchen for a bit of a sit-down & write this.

LATER

Miss D. found me there—still barking—& sent me outside saying 'Fresh sea air is what you need, Nancy! I can vouch that Oxcoombe air is ~~exsept~~ excepshunally healthy.'

I was going to take a turn along the bay. That's when I saw Mrs Shanto again. She came trotting out of a little low cottage just across the lane from the entrance gates. (She must keep a close eye on those gates.) Got a parcel in her hands—the brown paper all ripped down one side. 'This came for the Grange' she said. 'I kept it for you—&

the note inside. Got torn in the post.'

Not sure I beleeve her. Like Miss Dearing said—she is a funny old sort. And now Mrs Shanto knows that the new Housekeeper of Oxcoombe Grange used to work on a market stall!! And wears flesh-pink vests knitted by her grandma!

I walked away from her with all the dignity I could muster & found myself in the lane leading back to the village. So I had a look around. Oxcoombe's nothing much. Just a scatter of cottages & an old church on a hump with the stream running below it. There's only one other big house, on the far side & up the hill. All white walls & tall windows—looks new. Not 100-years-old new neither! I found a shop too. But the sign on the door was turned to CLOSED & nothing in the window but tins of Coleman's Mustard & a dead bluebottle.

Ella told me it was sleepy—but it was truly quiet as the grave. **LIKE A DESERTED VILLAGE!!** Then I saw a few curtains twitch & felt HIDDEN EYES UPON ME. It made my shoulders shiver to be watched like that. But I know what Aunty Bee would say: 'Nothing better to do than spy on the naybours? Nosey old biddies! Get back to your knitting!'

I kept on going along the lane just to get away from the prying eyes. I passed a farmyard & came to an old watermill with a board in the hedge saying:

TEA GARDEN * CREAM TEAS * BAKERY

It isn't the season for tea in the garden but nobody had taken it down. I leaned over the gate to just to take a peep—but it swung open & I tumbled in! I couldn't help it. Inside was a courtyard full of fallen leaves and iron chairs & tables piled up against the wall. Someone began shouting at me tho I was only getting up & dusting myself off! Couldn't properly make out the words but it sounded like 'No bread! No bread!' A door flew open and a woman's head poked out—all wild hair & red eyes & a big handkerchief held to her nose. She flapped her spare hand like somebody shooing birds & screeched 'No bread! Not today. Keep <u>away</u>.' Next instant the door slammed shut—& I heard a great sneezing fit going on inside.

Talk about feeling unwelcome!

I <u>ran</u> back here to the Grange—not out of fright—only in case I had spent too long Taking The Air. Let those nosy old biddies think what they liked. They're a FUNNY LOT in Oxcoombe. I don't beleeve I shall be making a great many friends here.

9. I INTEND TO KEEP NOTES

NANCY'S JOURNAL

I was glad to get back. The kitchen was nice & warm & Miss Dearing had put something in the oven that smelled good. I was just telling myself life here wasn't that bad & I was probbly making SOMETHING OUT OF NOTHING (as Gran would say) when there was another Mysterious Noise!

Again there was nobody but myself to hear it. Miss Dearing had driven off with Pancho on some errand. The afternoon was drawing in & I knew Mr Oakapple had retired to his tool-shed cos I saw the small glow of a lamp in there. Who knows where Peg was? Gone home I suppose. Tho I don't know where it is she lives.

Suddenly in all that eerie quiet there came a right LOUD THUMP & it made the dishes on the dresser jump—as well as me—so I couldn't have imagined it this time.

I sat very still and listened. There came a tiny creak from somewhere. Nothing after that. I sat like a statue for a bit longer. Then—as all was SILENT—I got up & crept about trying to make out where the noises came from. 'Use your Common Sense Nancy,' I told myself. That's what Aunty Bee would say. Not 'What a silly great fuss! Ought to be ashamed of yerself,' as Grandma more likely would put it.

Which is when my Employer arrived to find me tiptoeing down the passageway trying the floorboards for creaks. I had to pretend I was testing the slippery-ness of the polish! (As if that is something which Housekeepers do.) I don't want her to think I am a Bag of Nerves & wonder if she was right to take me on. I'm sure she would explain the noise as 'Simply a Sea Breeze catching under the floor, Nancy!'. I dare say it's becos she's been here many times over the years & never seen or heard anything odd. Perhaps it IS just me? Perhaps I am the SENSITIVE SORT?

So, in case anyone thinks me Foolish or refuses to bileve me, I intend to keep notes about it all on a fresh page—& shall add any other Observations I may make. I will show it to Ella when she comes.

ODD OCKURRENCES
AT OXCOOMBE GRANGE

1. Appearance: Intruder.
Where: On main stairs.
When: On arrival with Miss D.
Evidence: turned out to be Japanese Worrier's
Suit of Armour—very deceeving to the eye.

2. Noise: A bump.
Where: Kitchen.
When: Alone.
Evidence: none.

3. Something flitting at the corner of my eye.
Where: Upstairs passages.
When: Alone preparing Miss Dearing's room.
Evidence: none.

4. Observed that the Villagers of Oxcoombe act v. odd,
nosy, unfrendly.

5. Noise: Thump (loud) followed by creak (quiet).
Where: Kitchen.
When: Alone.
Evidence: plates rattled

10. ANYTHING YOU NEED IN A BOOK

As Ella arrived back at The Green that evening she glanced towards Apple Cottage. All was unnaturally still. It only now occurred to her how much she would miss seeing Pancho looking out over his fence, and Miss Dearing in one of her bright-coloured costumes dashing about on some errand or good cause. Miss Dearing had been a fixture at The Green for as long as Ella had lived there. She wondered who would come next to Apple Cottage, but couldn't really picture anyone taking their place.

She was so busy thinking about this that she was outside her own garden before she noticed her father in the gateway. He was about to take their dachshund, Sausage, for a walk.

'I've absolutely *got* to find something out about local history!' she said, without even greeting him, only bending to pat Sausage on the head. 'We must have books on the subject. Where will I find them?'

Ella hadn't wanted to worry Nancy unduly, but did

think it was worth trying to find out more about the history of Oxcoombe Grange, and whether there were any rumours or reasons for it to feel spooky. Even if she was going to discount these triumphantly with science!

'Hello to you too, Ella,' Professor Otter replied, quite used to Ella's funny ways. 'Try the dining room, on the shelves to the left of the fireplace. Or the top landing. And possibly the back bathroom.'

Their house was a jumble of books; books on every subject, squeezed double-depth along shelves, heaped on tables and underneath them, stacked in teetering piles, lining every step and stair. Ella was always secretly impressed that her father knew where anything was.

'Thank you!' Off she dashed, leaving Sausage and Professor Otter to their walk.

'Is this for homework?' her father called back. 'You sound rather pleased, for once.'

'No, not homework, Father. Perish the thought. It's—um—a little experiment of my own devising.'

With that she dashed indoors on her quest, beginning at the top landing.

'You can find anything you need in a book.' That was Ella Otter's maxim.

Except that the local history books she had hunted up from round the house weren't helping her research. Not at all. She flicked pages rapidly with one hand while eating her supper with the other: egg-and-bacon pie, made by their excellent housekeeper, Mrs Prebble. It needed no knife and fork, so long as you weren't fussy about crumbs. 'It's an old shirt anyway,' Ella thought, dabbing greasy pastry flakes off her front.

Seabourne's Early Days, A Survey of Victorian Piers, Memories of Old Sussex, all proved useless. Ella slammed them shut and pushed them aside. *Long-Ago Walks With Farmer Fry* had no chapter headings or index so she was reduced to skimming through, glancing at the amateurish illustrations for clues about where the walks might be. Whoever Farmer Fry was he never went near Oxcoombe. Nothing helpful there at all.

The last book was *Old Sussex Churches*. Ella put down her egg-and-bacon pie and cracked open the stiff pages. The smell of dust and mildew rose out of them, overpowering the smell of pie. But something caught her eye: a small scratchy black-lined sketch of a church on a mound, a squat stone building with a square tower at one end. She recognised it! The caption read: *St Winfrith's, Oxcoombe, the 'Smugglers' Church'*. Ella quickly read the page before and the page after to see if there was more information. Nothing. Nothing at all about the village of Oxcoombe, let alone why it should be called the smugglers' church, and not one word about Oxcoombe Grange. She flung the book down in disgust, and picked up the remains of her slice of pie. But her fingers smelled of mildew now, which quite spoilt it.

11. IN THE MIDDLE
OF THE NIGHT

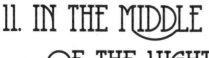

NANCY'S JOURNAL

I am sitting up in bed in my new room.

It's the middle of the night & I haven't had a wink of sleep. It feels like my ears are out on stalks & my eyes are peeled—every bit of me is ready to detect another Odd Ockurrence.

Not that anything <u>has</u> happened.

But I fear <u>it will</u>.

I wonder if a person who may be A BIT SENSITIVE is EVEN MORE SENSITIVE when they are just waiting for something to ockur?

Or does that drive away the thing that may be going to happen?

(I am trying not to think about that Thing.)

Courage, Nancy! I must try & be SENSIBLE. This scary feeling is all becos it is my 1st night here so everything feels very strange. The sounds or—to be exact—the <u>Silence</u>. The shape of the room. The size of the room. Bigger & higher than at home or at Miss Dearing's cottage. And how far away anyone else is. It feels like the distance from where I am to Miss Dearing's room is like walking the whole of

Bread Street! But Bread Street without a single soul in all the houses in between.

I wish this house wasn't <u>so vast</u>—or <u>so old</u>—or <u>so creepy</u>. I wish there was a fleet of butlers & footmen & maids to keep me company. I wouldn't mind being a lowly housemaid again cos then I'd have 2 or 3 other girls sharing this bedroom. And I wish someone like Mrs Prebble was the Housekeeper & took care of us all.

It doesn't help that Ella's words keep coming back to me. Not the ones about <u>logical reasons</u>—but saying Do you think the house could be haunted? Are there any stories about it?—as if other people in the past may have heard & seen the same things as me.

So I've kept the lamp on & I've got a torch beside me—the one Miss Dearing lent me to find my way to the privy back at Apple Cottage. I'm giving up on sleep. Instead I shall pass the hours by reading Lady Pouncey's <u>Guide to Household Management</u>. Lady P's idea of a household is very grand indeed. She favours heavy meals with a great deal of meat, which will not be happening here. Something tells me she is the sort who just LOVES giving orders!

It's a very DULL read—but that is the point. (I have stuffed 'Dark Deeds At Crag Castle' to the bottom of my suitcase—wrapped up in Grandma's vest!—& shoved the suitcase under the wardrobe.) There is not a speck of anything in Lady Pouncey to scare me. No chapter on 'Bumps In The Night' or 'Spooks On The Staircase'.

Tho there may be advice on How to Shine Up A Suit of Armour!

LADY POUNCEY'S GUIDE TO HOUSEHOLD MANAGEMENT

12. LIKE A GHOST MYSELF

NANCY'S JOURNAL

Phew—I got thru it but I don't want <u>every night</u> to be like that. And not a hint of an Odd Ockurrence to report! The sky is clear & the sun is up which makes me feel much braver—& a little bit silly. Everything looks so ordinary—& not at all creepy—in the sunshine.

Tho I admit I am not at my <u>most Observant</u> being half asleep. I look like A GHOST myself with a face as white as paper & big black smudges under my eyes. So much for the Sea Air doing me good like I said to Gran.

The new housekeeper

Miss Dearing is not very Observant either for she has not remarked on my appearance. She seems a bit pre-ocku-pied. I dare say there is still a lot for her to arrange. She talked at breakfast of getting Mr Oakapple to dig up a patch for a Kitchen Garden as 'We must have our vedgetables fresh out of the good earth'. Then she went outside to string up the washing line. I see she has tied one end to a tree clipped like a lollipop and the other round the neck of a statue of a naked man! I can't think Mr Oak will care for that when he finds it.

LATER

I've got the distinckt feeling that nobody (except Peg) really wants us here. All day as I dusted & swept those big gloomy rooms I've been turning it over in my mind. This is why I would make a good Detective if only someone would hire me. I can always come up with lots of Theories. (THEORY is a posh word for Idea & I knew it even before I met Ella Otter—who is full of posh words. And I can spell it!)

In this case, as follows:—
* They don't care for strangers (but peep at them round lace curtains)
* They don't like it when things change
* They were VERY VERY fond of Mr Duggan & don't

want anyone to take his place
* They don't like the look of Miss Dearing
* They don't like the look of ME! (That woman at the
  Tea Garden didn't.)
* They don't like Donkeys

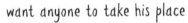

Then I had a better idea:—
* They wish Dominic Duggan had left the house to
  someone else (not Miss D.)
* That Someone Else still lives in the village
  & watched as our parade arrived
  & settled in . . .
* So who can that be?
* Miss Dearing told me her godfather had no children
  of his own to leave his money to. Her Dad was v. keen
  on getting Mr Duggan to be her godfather for that
  very reason. They were friends since schooldays—at
  some grand boarding school for boys. (Miss Dearing's
  brothers went there too but her Dad refused to spend
  any money on her education cos she was JUST A GIRL.
  She told me this story with un-dis-gized rage! 'I am
  still furious—even after 40 years!')
 *But what if Mr Duggan has a JEALOUS BROTHER
  OR SISTER still living? Tho surely Miss Dearing would
  have known this?

*Or what if he had a SECRET WIFE?

*That Tea Garden woman was certainly angry with me about something. Is SHE the sister or the wife?

* If the jealous brother or sister or secret wife doesn't live nearby they may well have A SPY in the village who reports back to them. One of those curtain-twitchers! Or somebody closer. Joshua Oakapple—or Mrs Shanto!

There's so many questions my head is spinning.

Now I've just thoght of another. Whoever—or Whatever—doesn't want Miss Dearing in the Grange:—
*Are they even FLESH & BLOOD?
*Or could they be acting from BEYOND THE GRAVE?

Now my spine is tingling as well as my head spinning. I'm tired & it's always easier to give in to bad thoghts at night-time. I'm going to put this Journal aside now & try not to think any more.

Oxcoombe Grange, Oxcoombe, Sussex.

Dear Aunty Bee,

I'm writing this PRIVATE note to you care of the Bus Depot cos I don't want to upset Dad or have Grandma say 'What's all this Nonsense?!'

But I must ask you—when I was younger did I ever show signs of hearing things that weren't there or seeing things that might be ghosts? I am sure I have always been quite the Common Sense type but I just wanted to inquire.

Trust me—it is nothing to worry about. I am settling in fine to my new position. This is a very big house with lots to do. But Miss Dearing my employer is as down-to-earth as you could wish. She is a Vedgetarian and spends her time on good works and rescuing donkeys.

Hope you are well (& wearing your winter vests!)

Your loving niece,

Nancy x

44 Bread Street, London S.E.

Dear Nancy,

The common sense type — that did make me chuckle! Your head has always been full of daydreams & dizzy ideas. Good for you, too! Who knows where life will take you if you THINK BIG?

But to answer your question, there's never been any sign that you are the Sensitive Type with a channel straight to the Supernatural. Have no fears on that ground. The only one in our family who leaned that way was my Granny — your Great-Grandma — who used to read the tea-leaves. One time she told me I was going to marry a dark handsome stranger & have three kids. So you can tell from that how good she was!

I can't help but worry, though. I hope you are not going the way of Mrs Boyd. Like so many grieving mothers since the War, it seems she has turned to Spiritualism. She goes to a weekly meeting at the Drapers Hall in the High Street, in the hope of hearing from their Billy. It may sound cruel but poor Billy Boyd was lost in the mud of France & won't be dropping into the Drapers Hall, no matter how hard his mother wishes it. She would do better to look after the ones

she's still got, Mr Boyd and poor Ethel. These Spiritualists &
Mediums are wicked, just battening on sad folk, if you want
my opinion.

As for your employer—she does not sound like Bread Street's
idea of down-to-earth. But you are mixing with all sorts now
and must learn to find your way.

Affectionately,

Your Aunty

13. TRUCULENT CHILD

'I do not expect to see Third Formers in my office. I certainly do not expect to see them twice.'

Ella was in front of the Deputy Head again; and again Miss Chard glared over the top of her spectacles. The stuffed owl looked on inscrutably. If it had heard similar words many times before it was not going to give the game way.

Miss Chard opened a drawer and took out an essay: Ella's essay, which she had forgotten all about.

Miss Chard lined up the pages and tapped them on her desk. She said, 'You are proving to be quite the most truculent child in the Lower School. I instructed you to write two pages on The Importance of Rules. What did you give me, Eleanor Otter?'

'An essay discussing the importance of rules, Miss Chard.'

'Discussing. *Discussing*.' Miss Chard made it sound almost like *disgusting*. Ella opened her mouth and sucked in a quick breath to speak but Miss Chard raised a hand, palm outwards, to stop her.

'You were not required to discuss the pros and cons.

This is not the Debating Society. You were not asked to write five-and-a-half pages. Now please go back and write me precisely two pages—no more and no less—on why school rules are right and proper, and I do not wish to see the words *silly* or *stupid* or *unnecessary* or *pointless* anywhere in your work. Do you understand?'

'Yes, Miss Chard. But I do think debating the subject has a— '

The palm was raised again, firmly.

'Never, repeat *never*, answer back to a grown-up.'

Ella screwed up her face. Her father—who was, after all, a professor—had always encouraged her to discuss and debate, and never to accept everything grown-ups said without giving it careful consideration. She was quite willing to discuss this with Miss Chard right now. She glanced at the owl. The symbol of female wisdom seemed to be raising its eyebrows. (Do owls have eyebrows? Ella wondered.) She decided it might be wiser on this occasion to stay silent.

'On my desk by tomorrow morning.'

'Yes, Miss Chard.'

'Go.'

'Yes, Miss Chard.'

A pause. There was one question, one burning question she just had to raise.

'There *is* something I'd like to ask, Miss Chard. I'd like to ask why it is wrong to take off a school hat, even when almost home, but not at all wrong to sneak on someone who has taken off their hat. Taking off a hat is morally neither here nor there. Sneaking on someone is. I would think that sneaking on others is not a quality to be encouraged in the young.'

'Eleanor Otter! I shall be speaking to your form teacher—and possibly your father—about your grievous tendency to insubordination.'

Ella said nothing. She slipped out of the room, making sure to close the door behind her without any hint of a slam. As she did so she took one last look at the owl. It stared straight back at her as if to say, 'What did you expect?'

Ella heard a cheer and looked up from her essay. The library where she was working was on the school's top floor and its windows had a perfect view of the playing fields. An inter-school hockey match was underway and a number of Third Form girls had stayed to watch, standing along the boundary of the pitch in straggly lines. Some of them were mad about hockey and some were just mad about Juniper Vale.

The cheer was for a goal and Ella could make out a fair-headed girl waving her hockey stick in triumph. Knots of girls on the sidelines jumped up and down and flung their arms about each other's necks. Honestly, Ella thought, I can't see what all the fuss is about. But she didn't stop watching.

Juniper Vale ran gracefully, her chin raised, her blonde hair flying back in the wind. She looked every bit the heroine. When she next whacked the ball it shot across the pitch and hit a player from the opposing team. Even Ella heard the crack of ball on bone. The girl went down like a tree toppling. Spectators squealed and gathered round, and the games mistress rushed over.

Juniper stayed where she was, carelessly brushing back her hair with one hand. She said something to a team mate, and laughed. So much for fair play, Ella thought. Juniper was just like her mother, happy to knock aside anyone who got in her way, and ignore the consequences.

Ella sighed and pushed the pages of her essay away. Exactly two pages. Bother The Importance of School Rules! She wished she could study the likes of Juniper Vale and discover why they had to be horrid when they were so blessed. That would be a much more useful topic for Miss Chard to read about.

14. GETTING ORGANIZED

NANCY'S JOURNAL

I used to bileve the FOLK IN CHARGE just gave orders & everything happened like clockwork. My last employer was like that. But Miss Dearing is a Different Kettle of Fish & things don't always go her way. Seems she wanted Mr Oakapple to turn the Cro-kay Lawn into a paddock for the donkeys. But he told her it wasn't his job. His job, he said in NO UNCERTAIN TERMS, was to look after the gardens not the livestock. Mr Duggan had promised him that he would be <u>kept on</u>. He wasn't the Estate Carpenter—or a Groom—or a mere Farmhand, he was Head Gardener. (Not that there is anyone else to be head of!)

Poor Miss Dearing was quite adjitated as she recounted this. I suppose it all comes from not having had to deal with Servants before & being too soft-hearted.

The style of garden Mr Oak keeps is very <u>orderly</u>. Which means hedges clipped in straight lines. Lawns like bowling greens. (In fact one of them is a bowling green.) He is not a great one for flowers—nor was Dominic Duggan apparently. So they suited each other just perfect. Now Peg has set up the old chicken run on the top terrace & there's ducks diving in the Lily-pond & geese mucking up the grass. Not to menshun that Goat which I've seen nibbling at the hedges. Must say I can't help but feel a <u>bit</u> <u>sorry</u> for Mr Oak.

Miss Dearing said 'I wonder if I can get the Shanto boys on to it? <u>They'd</u> do what I asked—and be glad of the work too.'

'The Shanto boys, Miss—who's that?' said I. But I had a sinking feeling about the reply & I was right: Mrs Shanto's sons—neither turned 20 yet—they pick up odd jobs where they can on farms & such. But harvest's in now so they are probbly looking for work. Seems their Dad had a fishing boat but he drownded years ago. 'Poor Mrs Shanto' Miss Dearing said & let out a sigh. 'Such a HARD LIFE.'

I was keen to hear more but Miss Dearing was expecting Mr Lubbock from the Garage. She wants to sell Dominic Duggan's old car. She dashed out leaving me here on my own again. I decided I mustn't FALL PRAY TO WORRIES but just be sensible & get on with my job. I must say that reading Lady Pouncey has given me a few tips on what a Housekeeper's actual Duties are. Like keeping the keys to everything lockable in the household (& keeping them locked!) & making sure your Store Cupboards are <u>perfectly</u> <u>organized</u>. I decide to follow her advice & organize my stores properly. Starting with the pantry.

Apart from what came from Apple Cottage there was nothing much in there to organize! Mr Dominic Duggan must have been a very poor eater—sometimes people are when they are old. Or a very greedy type who just ate everything up. Can't tell which. In the pantry all I found was ½ a jar of pickled colliflower and a pot of jam with fur on top. (At home jam never lasts us long enough to go mouldy like that.) There were a great many shelves with a great many sticky rings on them where THINGS HAVE STOOD in the past. All I could do was a get a stool & a cloth & wipe them all clean.

Then I looked in the Coal Hole. There didn't seem to be scarce more than a bucketful left & a lot of glittery black dust. Yet I haven't used all that much. This looks suspishus if you ask me! I made double-sure to lock every cupboard after me & tie my keys to my belt.

So since there was no more I could organize I sat down & wrote this Journal. I'm in such a hurry to get this down before Miss D. comes back that my writing looks all

I just heard another bump!

I swear this time it was underneath me.

I felt the floorboards jump. (I know Mr Oakapple said you must expect old floorboards to creak and pop but this was more.)

Not a creak or a pop.

It was a definite THUMP.

15. HIDING FROM THE BOGEYMAN

NANCY'S JOURNAL

LATER

(Now my handwriting has recovered!)

I am not making this up. I am not hearing things. I decided to BE BRAVE—& what's more—LOGICAL & see what could have made the noise. (Other than something Un-natural.)

- **What is under the kitchen?**
- **Does the house have a cellar?**
- **Or is it just solid earth?**
- **Are there pipes down there?**
- **Do pipes make that kind of noise?**

There was no ordinary cellar door to be seen in the kitchen so I started hunting for a trapdoor. I was just looking beneath the big kitchen table when a voice I knew said 'Miss Nancy Parker! What are you doing under there? Hiding from The Bogeyman?'

Bogeyman? I ask you!!

I crawled out—not looking very dignifyed—and tried to straighten everything: hair, cuffs, skirts. There he stood, bold as brass—Alfred Lubbock—the only person I knew who could get away with saying such things. Anybody else would be given a clip round the ear. But Alfred has such a breezy tone & blameless smile it seems no one ever takes him amiss.

I wish I was not so quick to blush. Also that flaming cheeks & ginger hair did not go so bad together. It's not that I'm sweet on Alfred or anything like that. It was just a supprise to find him in my kitchen. Specially when I was intent on finding a burglar—or a ghost!!

'Well, you are hardly the smart fellow I remember!' I said (in a VAIN ATTEMP at being droll) & to change the subject. I knew Alfred when he was the driver at my last place in Seabourne. For that job he had the nattiest uniform with tall shiny boots & a peaked cap. Now he wore greasy overalls made for a larger man & his hair stuck up as if he'd run his hands thru it. Plus his hands were filthy with oil & grime. 'What are you doing here?'

He said 'I've been under that motor out there in the coach-house. It's in good shape—well, it is now! Uncle thinks your Miss Dearing oughter keep it.' I'd forgot that Alfred's uncle was the same Mr Lubbock who runs the garage in Seabourne. Alfred went on 'Oxcoombe is so far from everywhere & she cannot expect old Pancho and the cart to get her about. Winter's coming too.'

Alfred went into the Scullery to wash & called out 'I'm often in the village. My Ma lives here. You must call on her. She'd like that.'

I nodded—thinking that if his mum was anything like Alfred she'd be good to get to know. Maybe behind those lace curtains they weren't ALL SO PECULIAR.

'You'll find her at the Mill. She runs a tea garden in summer and bakes the village bread all year round.'

The woman who shouted at me to go away? Oh dear, now I didn't know what to think! Except that she is certainly not <u>Mr Duggan's Sister or his Secret Wife.</u>

Before I could speak Miss Dearing stepped in from the yard with Mr Lubbock & Peg in hopes of a cup of tea. As I poured I said—very quietly—to Peg 'You know these Shanto boys who are going to save the day then?' Just 2 big useless lummoxes, according to her. But they will do anything for money. 'Can they put up a fence? A strong one?' I asked. She pulled a sour face. She never says much does Peg.

Afterwards I swirled the tea leaves in my cup & looked at the shape they made. (Don't really know what I'm looking for.) It could have been a DAGGER. It could have been a CLAW. Or maybe it was just an ARROW pointing to the sink & the washing up!

ODD OCKURRENCES AT OXCOOMBE GRANGE (WITH NEW OBSERVATIONS)

1. Appearance: Intruder.
Where: On main stairs.
When: On arrival with Miss D.
Evidence: turned out to be Japanese Worrier's Suit of Armour—very deceeving to the eye.

2. Noise: A bump.
Where: Kitchen.
When: Alone.
Evidence: none.

3. Something flitting at the corner of my eye.
Where: Upstairs passages.
When: Alone preparing Miss Dearing's room.
Evidence: none.

4. Observed that the Villagers of Oxcoombe act v. odd, nosy, unfrendly. But Alfred Lubbock's mum is one of them! Maybe I ran into her on A BAD DAY!

5. Noise: Thump (loud) followed by creak (quiet).
Where: Kitchen.

When: Alone.
Evidence: plates rattled.

6. Pantry: Food gone missing??
Evidence: rings where jars stood.

7. Coal store: Coal gone missing.
Evidence: my own eyes!

8. Noise: Definite <u>loud</u> thump.
Where: Beneath Kitchen floor (Cellar??)
When: Alone.
Evidence: none—interrupted in my search.

16. THE SHANTO BOYS

NANCY'S JOURNAL

Today I met the Shanto boys—they're not as useless as Peg said (or as they look). They are called Ears & Spud. I dare say that's not what their mother christened them but you can see why.

They've put up a great ugly fence round the Cro-kay lawn & are making another on the Bowling Green. Miss Dearing is <u>as pleased as pie</u>. Mr Oakapple on the other hand had a face like thunder when they showed up & seems to have made himself scarce.

I've been dusting in the Library (a job I think I shall NEVER finish.) It overlooks the lawns so I could keep an eye on those boys.

<u>What I observed:</u>—

* Spud gives the orders
  so I think Spud is the older brother
* Ears takes the orders & is not so clever
  on account of him stopping & rubbing his head at some of Spud's orders
* tho not all Spud's ideas <u>worked</u>—there was cursing!
* Spud makes jokes & Ears just grins

All in all it was quite a Pantomime. But I was supprised to see how quick the fences went up. (Must add I did not spend my <u>whole day</u> peering out the windows!)

Miss Dearing asked me to keep Ears & Spud plied with regular tea & a plate of her Shortbread Slices. They never said much to me—just nodded—& Spud Shanto winked. (Cheek!)

I took some to Peg as well. She looked a fright as usual but I must say I did admire her fingerless mittens. Each one had a big flower sewn on the back—one flower was pink & the other orange. The mittens were green. She kept them on while she held her cup of tea. I told her 'If I can take tea out to those Shantos I can bring some for you' & got such a funny look from her. She does not like them at all. Under her breath she said 'They'd rather have beer.' But Miss Dearing does not HOLD WITH DRINK so Darjeeling Tea will have to do.

I wonder if Gran would knit me some gloves like that?

Oh—I should put there has been <u>nothing spooky</u> to report today!

Dear Nancy,

I'm scribbling this quickly to say that I had hoped to come and see you at the Grange on Sunday but Father is taking me out for a treat. He says that I need cheering up. If he'd only let me abandon that wretched school I would be cheerful every day! Rest assured, I am thinking all the time about our investigation.

Your friend,

Ella Otter

P.S. If you come across any more strange occurrences: remember, think <u>scientifically</u>.

17. GOOD HUNTING

Professor Otter's idea of a treat was to visit a ruined abbey and then call on another professor for tea. Many years ago he had left his small town in America, which he felt was much too *new*, to study archaeology in England; and he never tired of looking at heaps of old stones. In the ordinary run of things Ella would have enjoyed the outing, but today she felt as if it was wasting precious time.

The abbey was in the middle of a farmer's field. Low ruins of walls were barely visible through their covering of brambles and shaggy grass. They marked rooms and doorways and passages, all meaningless to Ella. She would have learned something if she had listened to her father, but she was too busy thinking, 'I could be at Oxcoombe, looking for clues and questioning people!' She scrambled up the remains of a stone archway and watched the afternoon sun drop down behind the trees. At last her father signalled that it was time to go. She shivered and jumped down.

When they reached Professor Goring's house, Ella discovered that his study reminded her of home. Perhaps all professors' houses were the same. It was cluttered with books and papers and curious bits and pieces, and smelled of pipe tobacco and woodsmoke from the fire. Mrs Goring brought Ella a pile of children's books to look at. They were much too young for her but Ella sat politely thumbing through, with half an ear to the adults' conversation. They were talking about the abbey.

Professor Goring said, 'When Henry VIII had the religious houses closed down, some—the choicest sites—were handed over to his friends and made into private homes. Some, however, were destroyed outright. Others were allowed to fall into ruin. In either case that was not quite the end of them. Their stones were scavenged for building materials by the local people. Now *that*, young lady,' he said, trying to include Ella, 'would be an interesting occupation: trying to spot ancient stones and beams and tiles that have been carried off and incorporated into newer buildings.'

'It sounds fascinating,' Ella replied, glad to find that Professor Goring didn't think she was just a child, 'but I'd have to find a site near home.'

Mrs Goring came back in with a plate of crumpets to toast on the fire, followed by a maid with the tea tray. They had to step carefully round Professor Goring, who was rifling through the bookshelves in vague sort of way.

'Something about that here . . . where is it . . .?' he muttered, but before he could find what he wanted something else distracted him. 'Look at this, Otter, ever seen anything like that before?'

He held up a stunted, bulgy clay figure of a horse, not much bigger than his hand, which looked to Ella as if it had been made by a small child; a ham-fisted one at that. Professor Otter took it and turned it about, examining the figure closely. 'Interesting,' he said, in a tone that showed it *wasn't* a clay model made by a child. 'Not my area of expertise at all. But I can see it's very old. Where did you get it?'

'Some chap who deals in antiquities. Bale? Bailey? He keeps a shop not far from the British Museum—that's where I saw it, in the window. From ancient Greece, he says, the chap.' Professor Goring chuckled. 'It's far from *my* area of expertise, too!'

'If only you stuck to what you knew about, dear,' Mrs Goring teased him, and glanced at Ella to see if she agreed. But Ella felt strongly that she was on the professor's side, and refused to smile simperingly back.

Her father handed her the figure. Looking closely, she could see that it wasn't some clumsy childish attempt. Its bulges matched on both sides, its sturdy legs and neck showed the animal's strength. She returned it to Professor Goring who set it carefully back on a shelf.

'Now, where was I? Ah, yes.' He pulled down an old book and flicked through the roughly-cut pages. 'Where do you live again, Otter? Seabourne, is it? Yes, yes, there was an old priory, just a small community, at a place called Oxcoombe. Sold to Sir William de Warne.' He turned to Ella with a big smile, showing off his snaggled teeth. 'Oxcoombe's not far from Seabourne. Good hunting!'

It was quite dark by the time they got on the train home. Ella gazed out of the window. Her reflection, yellowish and hollow-eyed in the dirty glass, gazed back. The tiresome treat had proved most fortunate in the end, better than she could ever have expected. An old priory at Oxcoombe, seized and sold to one of King Henry's friends, while its monks were thrown out and abandoned to their fate. Rebuilt as a private house . . . perhaps the shade of an angry prior or a miserable monk still haunted it? It had to be Oxcoombe Grange. Unless there were other large houses there? She had serious investigating to do. Good hunting, indeed.

18. JUST LIKE GOLDILOCKS

NANCY'S JOURNAL

I spoke too soon when I put 'Nothing to Report'!

Miss Dearing decided to take her supper in the Dining Room. She says she's the Lady of Oxcoombe Grange now & ought to act like it. Talk about fuss & bother—there's no one to know but me! (Not that I call putting up a washing line v. ladylike.) She cooked most of the meal herself but I had to carry the dishes thru. It took a while to get them from the kitchen & down the hallway, growing colder all the time. To my mind Miss D. looked very sad sitting there <u>all alone</u> at the end of that great long table. Like Goldilocks after she stole into the Bears' house—if the Bears' house was hung about with the heads & hides of other creatures they had captured & eaten!

Once I served the pudding (apple pie) she said—all very grand— 'I shall take coffee in the Drawing Room Nancy.'

The Drawing Room faces the sea & gets all the weather thrown at it. Those tall windows are full of gaps & drafts. I hadn't lit the fire in there—only laid it—not knowing she would want to be in there too. So I quickly put a match to the fire (quite a few matches in fact as the sea air makes everything DAMP) & lit the lamps & drew the curtains. It still felt <u>far from Cosy</u>.

When I came back with the coffee—I can make that—Miss Dearing was huddled up close to the fire with a box of chockolates open on a footstool. 'Do have one,' she said—much more like the old Miss Dearing. So I did. Lady Pouncey <u>would not</u> approve. In that book of hers she is VERY FIRM on the subject of Relations between Master & Servant.

Back in the kitchen I sat warming my feet on the oven door. I was just dozing off—on account of <u>never</u> sleeping well at night—when the Drawing Room bell rang.

Miss Dearing looked supprised. I said 'You rang for me Miss' and she said 'No I didn't.' I said 'You did Miss,' and she said 'Indeed I did not' and this went on a bit until she said I must be HEARING THINGS.

Oh this is a great house for hearing things! Except it is only <u>me</u> that <u>does</u>.

I hurried back to examine the bells—which are in the passageway just outside the kitchen—and what should I trip over in the hallway?

A HEAD!! A chopped-off head!

It went flying off my shoe & bounced on the bottom stair. The hallway's quite dingy so I didn't know it was a head at first. I had to bend down (with shaking hands & pounding heart) & see what on earth I'd kicked:—

Some kind of pig—but not any pig's head you'd see in the butchers. It must have fallen off the wall. When I looked up I could see the gap.

Then the Drawing Room bell rang again! I went back this time wondering if it would be another NO I DIDN'T! YES YOU DID! talk—but Miss Dearing was there all saucer-eyed saying 'Did I hear a scream Nancy?'

'You may have Miss' I replied. 'There is a head on the hall floor.'

'A HEAD??' she said looking even more like poor little Goldilocks scared stiff by the Bears coming home.

'A wild pig—but very dead. Fallen off the wall. One of

Mr Duggan's soo-veneers.'

Miss Dearing fanned herself with a newspaper & said 'I wundered if you were going to say a mouse's head—something a cat might bring in.'

'We haven't got a cat' I reminded her. She agreed. Then she said it was very likely the pig fell off of the wall cos the plaster was rotten—the nail was broken—the head had shrunk—or we had DISTURBED it with all our Comings & Goings.

None of those reasons convinced me. I don't think they convinced Miss Dearing neither. She looked quite shaken. I wish Miss D. did hold with strong drink as we might have had a nip of Brandy like my Gran ~~recko~~ reckermends for A BAD SHOCK. Instead I left her to her coffee—cold by now.

I still had to check the bells. I put my hand to the wire of the Drawing Room bell & it tinkled. I did it again. There was nothing to show whether or not the bell had truly rung before or WHO—or WHAT—had rung it.

So I crept back to my warm place by the Excelsior & got out this Journal. I cannot say my writing is very steady.

ODD OCKURRENCES AT OXCOOMBE GRANGE (CONTINUED)

Latest events:—

9. Mysterious ringing of Drawing Room bell!

10. Pig's head fell off wall of its own accord!!

There is definitely <u>something scary</u> going on.

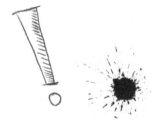

19. AS GOOD AS A
MOULDY CABBAGE

NANCY'S JOURNAL

I think me & Miss Dearing both had a DREADFUL NIGHT, but Alfred appeared bright & early this morning to take her for a driving lesson—which gave us both something else to think about.

Miss D. has given in to Mr Lubbock and decided to keep the motor car. I just can't picture her driving it. Normally she is very peaceful—but when she gets in that donkey cart waving her whip at other ~~vickuls~~ veerculls— she reminds me of Britannia on a Penny coin with her trident & her big cart-wheel. (Aunty Bee says it's a shield but it always looks like a cart-wheel to me.)

So then—whether I wanted to or not—I got sent off to visit Alfred's Mum. I must say even if Miss D. does not give actual orders she can get you to do something just by Being Very Nice. 'You've not had your Day Off yet. We must make amends for that,' was what she said. But somehow my free time turned into calling on someone else's mother. 'Ma's been out of sorts lately' Alfred said. 'She'll be glad to see a cheery face.' I don't know how he could think my face is cheery when I'm looking my very worst!

I was nervous knocking on Mrs Lubbock's door. Last time it flew open & somebody furious told me to Go Away! I was hoping that wasn't actually Alfred's mum—but I reckernised her right off as the same woman. Except there was nothing cross or peevish about her today. Only a sniff remained.

'Do come in.' She quickly took off her apron & stuffed it somewhere while showing me into the Parlour. 'Alfred has TOLD ME ALL ABOUT YOU.' When someone says that I get a quaking feeling inside. What have they told? Good or bad? I was just wundering when she peered a bit closer.

'Oh dear! Forgive me Miss Parker' she said. (Miss Parker indeed!) 'It was you that called the other day. I must apple apollergise. You see—I was feeling so poorly I couldn't bake at all—& I did not want to pass on my germs.'

Just then the mantel-clock struck the ½ hour & Mrs Lubbock jumped up again saying 'Rolls' & dashed away. I called out that I didn't mean to bother her if she was busy. I heard a bang & a crash so I ran thru the kitchen & into the bakehouse—ended up helping her rescue a vast tray of hot rolls. 'No bother at all' she said & grinned at me. Now I know where Alfred gets his easy-going ways from.

Once we had the rolls safe & cooling on racks Mrs Lubbock made some tea but we never went back to the parlour. We sat in the kitchen in a frendly way & she TOLD ME ABOUT HER & Alfred. It's all a bit like another fairy tale (everything in Oxcoombe is!) —the miller & his wife & child.

Mrs Lubbock is a widow. Her husband was the miller & ran the bakehouse with another man to help. They went off to War & she took over—tho she couldn't run the Mill on her own & Alfred was too young. 'Besides he always cared more for engines than for baking' she said. These days the flour arrives by the sackful from another mill. But she still bakes bread & says she can bring a loaf to the Grange every morning. Since I have not yet mastered Pastry—let alone Bread—I was glad to hear that. In summer she runs the Tea Garden too.

'I had a girl helping me with that but now she's gone to your Missus I don't know what I shall do next year. Peg Shanto,' she said & made a sad little face.

Peg Shanto??!! I may have raised my voice at that part.

Mrs Lubbock certainly looked supprised.

'She's a Shanto?' I asked when I got myself settled again.

Oh yes, she is—and now I feel such a FOOL. (Again.) Ears & Spud are her brothers—tho she didn't own up to it and called them great lummox—& funny old Mrs Shanto is her mum. Why did I not spot this? Why did nobody say? Not even Miss Dearing! I fear as a Detective I am as good as a mouldy cabbage is good for Sunday dinner.

'She'll be better tending animals than tending customers' Alfred's Ma said. So TRYING to be more detective than cabbage I wundered aloud about Peg. Now I know:—

1. She does not get on with her brothers

2. She does not get on with her mum

3. Mrs Lubbock calls her the <u>White Sheep of the family</u>! Tho she would not say why.

4. No one can hardly get a word out of her (which I knew already) (and which is why Mrs Lubbock found her not as useful as may be with the Tea Garden)

5. But she is straight & ~~onest~~ honest & has a GOOD HEART.

So then I didn't feel quite so stupid. It's Peg herself who's been keeping quiet about being a Shanto.

I did say to Mrs Lubbock that I admired Peg's knitted gloves. I saw her give me a look then—thinking how Peg & me could be frends. 'You 2 girls are not far off in age. There's preshus few young people in Oxcoombe,' she said.

I longed to ask Mrs Lubbock lots more but she had to get on. Besides it does not do for a Detective to give away what they're after.

20. SHANTOS EVERYWHERE

NANCY'S JOURNAL

I wrote all that last bit sitting on the beach. I was down behind a big rock for shelter but the pages still kept blowing about. It's not such a bad life when you can sit beside the seaside on your Day Off! Tho by the time I finished my hands were freezing. (Need some fingerless gloves like Peg's.)

Came back here to find Spud Shanto hammering away at a new hen-house. The hens were cowering in their old run—the one that came from Apple Cottage & went a bit crooked when it was set up here. This new one will be A PALACE by the looks of it. The hens aren't too bad cos they're kept in their run—so far. But the ducks & geese have made a right old mess of the Lily-pond Lawn. The grass has turned to mud & there's feathers everywhere. Not to mention goose droppings. Reminds me of the garden—if you can call it that—at Apple Cottage.

Then I went indoors & Ears was up a tall ladder nailing that Pig's Head back on the wall.

There are Shantos everywhere about the Grange (now I know Peg is their sister.) I suppose they have lived on the doorstep for years. It's like me & the Biscuit Factory—it looms over Bread Street & half the neybourhood works there & we all breathe in the smoke of its chimneys. I dare say they're expecting their tea & cake now. But it's still my Day Off so I came up to my room & read bit more Lady Pouncey. She hasn't got much to say about servants & time off except that 'It may be sacrificed if staff are required about the house'. Which means YOUR TIME IS NEVER YOUR OWN—even when it's your free time!

I tried to ask Ears Shanto about that Pig's Head. Was the plaster cracked or rotten? Did the nail fall out? He just looked down from his ladder & gave me a daft grin.

He was up close to some kind of deer with long curly horns. I wouldn't care if he got spiked by them. But I tried again. Was it all the moving about upstairs that dislodged it? (Me running back & forth with cans of water & buckets of coal.)

His grin just got wider & more daft. 'Maybe' he said. 'Old place like this. Anything can happen.'

Well—that was helpful.

21. TRUSTWORTHY

Ella burst through the heavy door, her satchel banging against her hip and her *porridge pot* tipped over one eye. A slice of bracing sea air blew in with her. Straight ahead were the double glass doors to the town museum. To the right was a large room used for public meetings and lectures, and to the left was the lending library.

Ella knew the place well. She came here with her father, mostly to look round the museum so that he could show her how things *shouldn't* be done. 'Anteaters aren't usually that shape, Ella. It's just very badly stuffed.' Or, 'The date on that label is incorrect by a century.' Or, 'This information is not only incorrect, it is very badly worded—and the ink is smudged.' But Ella was fond of the museum with its random collection of exhibits, often donated by local residents, and liked it just as it was.

But today she took the left-hand entrance. The library was small and never very busy. In winter the librarian, Miss Valentine, doubled up as keeper of the museum, which was just as quiet once the holiday season was over.

Having so much time on her hands, Miss Valentine relished a challenge and Ella knew it. She said, 'I need to find out about Oxcoombe in the old days, please. For homework. It's urgent.'

Miss Valentine wiped her spectacles in preparation. 'Hmm, do you want books, or maps, or the newspaper of the day?'

'Everything!'

'The Reference Library is the place to start. You know that you can't take anything out of it, don't you? Have you brought paper for taking notes?'

Ella patted her satchel. Miss Valentine took a key from a desk drawer. She glanced around at the three or four people using the library, decided they could be trusted, and twitched her head, commanding Ella to follow.

The Reference Library was on the top floor, and the only way to reach it was a staircase at the back of the Museum. Miss Valentine unlocked the door and pointed Ella to the shelves and cabinets she needed.

'Do take care. Some of these old documents are fragile, and many are irreplaceable. Remember, we close at five.' She dangled the key in front of Ella's nose. 'Bring this back ten minutes beforehand, please. I would not trust another child in here alone, but since it's you, Ella Otter . . .'

Ella examined tiny print with her nose almost touching the paper. She gazed at old illustrations, ran her finger down columns of fine print, hoping to pick out certain words and names. Every so often her eyes gleamed and she lifted her pencil to make a note. It was like doing a jigsaw puzzle, fitting small pieces together.

The daylight was fading. The clock showed eleven minutes to five. Ella shuffled books back on to shelves, maps into drawers. Her hand paused on one crackled old document, wavering. Miss Valentine trusted her.

No one would ever know. No one else came up here. She could just 'borrow' it, and slip it back another day. In the meantime she would take utmost care of it. Of course Miss Valentine could trust her.

As she hurried down the hallway with the key a draught lifted a row of notices pinned to the wall. One in particular drew her attention.

A VERY RARE OPPORTUNITY
FOR RESIDENTS OF SEABOURNE

A Public Audience
with Madame Arcana
Psychic, Medium.

It was to be next week, in this very building. Ella's eyes widened. Again her mind went racing. It's a sign! she thought.

22. FOOTSTEPS

Ella had to run for the train home, and flung herself into the last door of the last carriage just in time. The guard slammed it shut and blew his whistle.

It was dark by the time she got off at Seabourne Halt. Deep shadows lurked between the pools of lamplight. At the far end of the train someone else climbed down, half-hidden in the swirling cloud of steam. Ella hurried away, knowing that she would have to walk up the narrow lane with a stranger's footsteps echoing behind her. For the first time she had an inkling of how Nancy must feel, alone in Oxcoombe Grange, jumping at shadows and sudden noises. It wasn't just a great lark, or a fascinating scientific experiment.

'Ella! Slow down!'

'Father?' Ella stopped, aware of her heart thudding under her ribs.

Professor Otter caught up with her. 'You're very late home. Not another detention, surely?'

Ella almost wished it had been, then her father would know how mean school continued to be. But she said, 'I've been at Seabourne Library, carrying out essential research.'

Professor Otter lifted his briefcase. 'And I've been up to the British Museum for a meeting with my friend Wapshott, who works in the Mediaeval Galleries. A very good day. How was school?'

Ella thought for a moment. She hadn't yet decided on her Word of the Day. The other girls had been full of the latest victory of the hockey team and wondering wildly whether Juniper Vale actually curled her hair. 'Today school was . . . insipid,' she said.

Maddeningly her father just chuckled.

They were coming to the end of the station lane. Ella said, 'Be careful. It's just here that Mrs Vale often shoots round the blind bend, nearly clipping the top off one's nose!'

'That dark red Daimler?'

'Precisely.'

'I think we're safe tonight. No sound of an engine, no headlights showing.' Professor Otter went on, 'I looked into that shop today. Do you remember? The one that Goring talked about, the dealer in antiquities.'

Ella nodded, even though her father couldn't really see her in the dark. She pictured the little clay horse she had held that was hundreds, if not thousands, of years old.

'Unfortunately it was shut. There were just two or three things on display in the window. But, most intriguing, the name above the door was Vale. Any connection with your road hog, d'you think?'

They turned on to The Green and welcoming lights

shone out from the houses all around.

'How could there be?' said Ella.

DEADLY SECRET!

Dear Nancy,

In the course of my initial researches I have already found out important information regarding our experiment. Will convey it to you in person, not on paper.

Of course, dratted school gets in the way! But I've just learned it is Founder's Day this week, which means a half-holiday. I can be with you on Thursday by the half-past twelve train.

E. Otter

23. MISS DEARING GETS A LETTER

NANCY'S JOURNAL

So tired last night that I slept like a log. A ghost could have come & leaned over my bed & still I would not have woken!

I wish I had not put that now. That horrible idea will stick in my head all day.

LATER

Another worrying thing has ockurred. Miss Dearing got a letter that upset her. When she opened it she said 'Not again!' & flung it into the Excelsior. Once it had been CONSUMED BY FLAMES she muttered 'Good riddance!' I acted as if I was Invisible. Just got on with clearing breakfast which Miss D. still eats in the kitchen. All the while my mind racing with the following Theories:—

* Can't be a LOVE LETTER. Miss Dearing is far too old for romance.

* Or final demand on A BILL. She is a good payer. All the tradesmen seem happy in their dealings with her.

* I suspect it was a nasty letter—one of those ANONYMOUSE ones—from some ill-wisher who dares

not put their name.

Which takes me back to my Theory that <u>somebody</u> does not want Miss Dearing in this house.

I ran outside. Mr Oakapple was sweeping a path. When I asked him if he'd seen anyone bring a letter he said 'You mean the postman? No. But he's in the habit of giving letters to me or Mrs Shanto—whoever's here—on account of nobody living at the Grange lately. Same in Mr Duggan's time cos he was away more often than not.'

I asked 'Seen anybody else?' but he shook his head & went back to sweeping.

(I have never spoke so much with Mr Oak before!)

(Of course it could be Mr Oak that wrote the nasty letter!! If he <u>blackmailed</u> Miss D. into getting rid of the animals he could go back to smooth clean lawns.)

Next I went to find Peg. She was in the yard with 2 donkeys I'd never seen before—brushing the smaller one down. She shook her head too & said 'Now now Little Jem' but she was only speaking to the donkey.

Just to prove Mr Oak's point—who should walk up then but Alfred's Ma with the post! She had a fresh loaf for Miss Dearing & a parcel addressed to:

Miss N. Parker, Housekeeper, Oxcoombe Grange.

I asked both her and Peg if they had seen anyone about but they shook their heads. Mrs Lubbock had to get on with delivering more bread—but I remembered what she said about Peg being the only girl here near my age. I always felt Peg was stand-off-ish but maybe I have not been so very frendly myself. So I waved my parcel & said 'Lovely! Books!! From my Aunty Bee!!! She always gets me books.'

(I may have sounded a bit too keen. Or just BARKING MAD.)

Not so much as a smile from Peg. She moved on to brushing down the other donkey. 'Don't like reading,' she muttered.

I tried again. 'I <u>do</u> admire those gloves of yours. Did your mum make them for you?'

Peg sort of grunted. 'Knitted them myself. The flowers are croshay-work.'

I told her 'When I tried knitting Socks-for-the-Troops at Sunday School they gave them back. There was always something wrong with them—so they said—baggy or lumpy & so on. Troops could not go to war in socks as bad as mine!'

Sure I saw the start of a smile then so I went on: 'Got any <u>other</u> brothers and sisters? I'm an ONLY myself.' If I'd known what was coming next I may not have grinned so wide.

Peg looked at her feet & said 'I had 2 more brothers—

older than Ears and Spud—killed in the war. Thumbs and Edward. Thumbs was short for All Fingers & Thumbs.' (Seems like Edward was the only one not to get a nickname.) 'I got on well with Edward—far & away the kindest . . .'

That is the longest speech she's made yet. But I felt so bad for her. I wanted to tell her my Dad was in the War & came back quite changed. To this day he's still not like himself—so quiet & turned in. But leastways he came back. So I kept this to myself. That is the Trouble with the War. It's over & done with now but it still hangs there like a BIG BLACK CLOUD. So all-in-all this has been a bit of a gloomy morning.

And I am not much nearer solving the puzzle of the letter. Of course it may be Peg who sent it. A Detective must not rule anything out! But that makes no sense cos if the donkeys & Miss Dearing go—she's out of a job. We all are.

Oxcoombe Grange, Oxcoombe, Sussex.

Dear Aunty Bee,

Just a v. quick note to say Thank You for the books.
I hope you shan't think me ungrateful but I must put
them aside for a bit. I found an old book on Household
Management which I am studying in spare moments.
Polishing up my know-how!!

You said I must tell my employer more servants are
needed for such a big house but it is not as easy as
all that for a girl my age. Besides Miss Dearing has
STRONG VIEWS. If I told you how many staff Lady
Pouncey would employ you would never beleve me!

Sending my love to Dad & Gran.

Nancy xxx

P.S. Lady Pouncey is the one that wrote the book on
Household Management.
P.P.S. Please don't worry yourself any more about my
enquiry regards Being Sensitive. That was probbly all
very silly & I am sure there is a logical explanation.

24. QUESTIONS FROM LADY POUNCEY

NANCY'S JOURNAL

I didn't tell Aunty Bee the truth about her books—they look a bit too GRIM & GRISLY for my taste right now. It's all very well reading about bloody murder when you can hear your Gran snoring the other side of the wall & can warm your cold feet on Aunty's. (The back-bedroom mattress at Bread Street is saggy & we always roll into the middle.) But <u>not</u> when you're all alone in a big creaky house with the only other soul at the furthest end from you.

It IS true I'm reading Lady Pouncey instead. I cannot say I like her—she sounds a right old Fusspot & a Bossy-boots & a Snob. But she's made me think. By her reckerning there should be at least 8 indoor servants for a place this size. Not just me! A Butler to look after the silver & the <u>wine cellar</u> & a boy for lamps, boots & knives ect. Then a Housekeeper & a Cook & maids.

Now my head is buzzing with questions for Miss Dearing:—

1. Does she truly expect me to keep this house clean & warm & tidy all on my own?

2. How did Mr Dominic Duggan manage?

3. I've heard that Mrs Shanto cleans houses in the village. Did she do some cleaning here?

4. Is that what Miss Dearing meant when she said Mrs Shanto kept an eye on the house?

5. Has Mrs Shanto got a set of KEYS?

6. Is Mrs Shanto fed up that she doesn't work here any more?

7. Is Mrs Shanto fed up with Miss Dearing?

8. Or with ME?

9. Did Mr Duggan or any of his servants notice any Odd Ockurrences?

10. Did he ever tell her any Strange Tales from the past?

11. Did Mr Duggan die in this house!?

12. Also Important—is there a wine cellar here? (Lady Pouncey says any Good Establishment requires one.) If that's where some of those noises are coming from, how do I get into it?

13. Then—do I dare say anything about the letter she threw in the fire?

But I don't want to get on Miss Dearing's nerves if she is still upset from that Anonymouse Letter. So I shall have to choose my time carefully. And that's 13 questions—13 is an unlucky number! —and <u>far too many</u> to ask.

25. BEING DISCREET

NANCY'S JOURNAL

Them that don't ask, don't get, as Aunty Bee says.

Miss Dearing was at the kitchen table showing me how to make a Mushroom Pie. (Same as Cottage Pie but no meat.) Cooking always puts her in a GOOD MOOD. So I asked—at least a bit—of what I wanted to know. I'll have something to tell Ella when she comes.

'To be quite truthful Nancy,' Miss Dearing said, 'I did not know my godfather particularly well. He was a very private man. I don't think he really <u>liked</u> people. He kept few servants for the time & turned them out when he went away. Except one butler-cum-valet who was with him for many years—went with him on his travels too—utterly loyal & discreet.'

(I gather that DISCREET means being careful about what you say. Not gabbing your master's bizzness to all & sundry.)

Thanks to Lady Pouncey I was on firm ground here. A Butler takes charge of the wine cellar & serves the drinks at grand dinners.

But Miss D. said 'Such ideas! My godfather hated house parties and grand dinners. I'd say he was almost a re-clouse.'

I wundered aloud what happened to the Manservant &

she said he got left some money in Mr Duggan's will. He came from overseas & went back there as far as she knew. Which means he is <u>not living nearby</u> full of RESENTFUL FEELINGS about what us new residents of Oxcoombe Grange get up to!!

So next I wundered—ever so ~~caz~~ cashual—where Mr Duggan died & it turned out Switzer-land! He was buried there too—up a mountain—which Miss Dearing said would make him very happy. So he did not keel over in the Dining Room or waste away a-bed upstairs! It is not <u>his restless spirit</u> I see flitting about in the shadows.

I had to press on about the Cellar so I asked direct if there was one in the house. But Miss Dearing did not know—& being opposed to Strong Drink she has no interest in keeping wine. I said 'Did you never go exploring, Miss—when you came here as a child?'

'Oh no! Victorian children were supposed to be SEEN & NOT HEARD—and only seen when the grown-ups chose. We did as we were told. In some places child visitors got taken to the kitchen for titbits—the staff liked to treat them as pets. Not here. The back parts of the house were a mystery to me.'

My next question was about Mrs Shanto. I made it sound like idle chit-chat as we worked. As if I didn't care about the answer. But all Miss D. said was 'Mrs Shanto can be a little nosy.' Then she added 'I'm glad to have Peg & I employ the Shanto boys as much as I can. There—this pie is ready to go into the oven now.'

Tho I had tried v. hard to be DISCREET myself—I got the distinckt feeling that Miss Dearing felt I had asked quite enough questions for one day!

44 Bread Street, London S.E.

My dear Nancy,

I trust you are settling in & doing your best. Enclosed is a lambs-wool girdle I knitted. You must wear it next to your skin, under your vest & petticoat. It will keep the cold off your kidneys. I made one for your Aunt Beatrice & she swears by it. That's a drafty old job she's got on the buses specially with this awful weather we've been having.

Remember what I always say — 'better be safe than sorry'.

From your ever-loving Grandmother

P.S. Ethel Boyd has got the Shingles now. I reckon she won't be out of bed this side of Christmas. She could probably do with a lambs-wool girdle too.

Oxcoombe Grange, Oxcoombe, Sussex.

Dear Gran,

Thank you very much for the girdle. If you are still in a
knitting mood I wonder if you could find the time to make
me some gloves? They would be very useful. I will try and
draw them below.

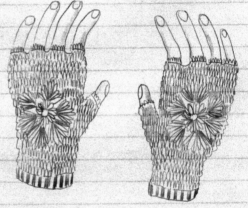

Sorry to hear about poor Ethel. I feel sure working on
the Fruit & Veg stall in all weathers is what has laid her
so low. I am very cosy here in the kitchen with a most
effishunt cooking range called the Excelsior to keep me
warm. What with that & my free time spent on healthy
seaside walks I have to say I am MOST IMPROVED.

Give my love to Dad & Aunty Bee.

Nancy x

26. FOR THE RIGHT MOTIVES

NANCY'S JOURNAL

I know it's wrong—but I did it for the best MOTIVES. I mean <u>steaming open</u> someone else's letters.

I've read all about it in stories so I knew what to do. You hold the stuck-down bit of the envelope in the steam from the kettle until it lifts up. Afterwards you can stick it back again without the person knowing.

What I found inside was another of those Anonymouse Letters. That's why what I did is <u>not really wrong</u>. I am saving Miss Dearing from FURTHER DISTRESS.

I was up early (those geese making a racket) and there was an envelope pushed under the front door. Just a single sheet inside. Someone had tried to ~~dig~~ dis-gize their writing by making it all crooked. Once I read it I could hardly seal it up again & pass it on like I knew nothing. Nor was I going to stuff it in the flames to destroy it. I am keeping it for <u>Evidence</u>.

I may not be the world's best Housekeeper but I beleeve I repay my employer for her kindness by being very LOYAL*. Except she must <u>never know!</u> Which is a bit annoying.

(*Not so sure about being DISCREET. Ella comes tomorrow & I shall certainly be talking things over with her.)

Utterly disgraceful!!

You have turned Oxcoombe Grange into a gypsy encampment. The ruination of a formerly elegant house and garden. Now every sight and sound is an abomination! Farm animals everywhere. Intimate clothing hanging in the garden for all to see. Noise and rabble. You are not fit to reside in such a place. A muddy hovel is your natural home. You should go back there and take your livestock with you!!

I repeat YOU ARE A DISGRACE.

Whoever it is they know some long words & I dare say have spelt them correcktly too.

My Theory as to the AUTHOR. It cannot be:—

—Mrs Shanto—I'm sure she never uttered words that big in her life. Nor if she put a pen to paper would it come out like that. (Unless that crooked writing is her ACTUAL TRUE HAND.)

—Mr Duggan's old servant for he is gone abroad.

—Well—that is where my Theory runs out as it could be just about anyone else! Who knows what sort of person lurks behind the lace curtains of Oxcoombe? There may be an educated lady down on <u>hard times</u>. Or an educated gentleman: one of those War Wounded who are a bit crazy after all THE HORRORS they went thru.

I must try & talk to Alfred's mum again. I shan't let on what I'm worried about, just make crafty inquiries. This needs investigating!

27. DAWN VIGIL

NANCY'S JOURNAL

I am keeping a Dawn Vigil. Been up since before dawn so if anyone's creeping about posting more Anonymouse Letters I will be the first to know about it! I'm hid between the Drawing Room curtains with just one eye peeping out so I should spot anybody coming up the path. Without them spotting me.

Keep looking back over my shoulder too—bit nervous of the shadows behind me.

All I can see as the day-light comes up is those grim old trees pointing their spiky fingers at the house. Nobody sneaking up the path. Nothing out of the ordinary.

But if another cruel letter comes I shall:—

• Know who brings it
• Keep it from getting into Miss Dearing's hands
• Keep it as further evidence

Surely it's AGAINST THE LAW to write such wicked stuff!

Tho I don't know what law—as it's true the donkeys & geese & goat ect. are making a wreck of the garden.

Glad I got Miss D. to send all the washing off to the laundry in Seabourne now. A smart grey van drove up & took it away & will bring it back clean & ironed too.

No more bloomers soaking in the scullery sink! Or sheets flapping over Mr Oakapple's blessed Parr-tair. (Which is a garden made up of short little hedges grown in a very fiddly pattern. It's best viewed from the upstairs windows—which Miss Dearing says was the point of it—but not if there's a droopy line of washing in the way.)

Still nobody in sight. Just a bird pecking the lawn.

Just heard <u>creaking</u> up above—creaks like footsteps.

Now they are going back & forth.

Most deliberate. Nobody creeping.

I just heard a door open & close.

Of course the Yellow Bedroom is above here-abouts. I reckern it's just Miss Dearing getting up! So I better run & get the hot water on.

28. HALF-HOLIDAY

'Nancy, I've so much to tell you!'

Ella burst into the kitchen at Oxcoombe Grange, out of breath from her long fast walk from the station. Then she stopped. The room was big and old-fashioned but orderly and clean, with copper pans hanging on one wall, and plates of all sizes arranged on the shelves of a huge dresser. It was also deliciously warm and smelled of baking. From what Nancy had said she was expecting something like a dungeon, with dirty cobwebs hanging in the corners!

'I've got lots to tell *you*,' Nancy replied. She glanced away and whispered, 'The latest? Bells ringing when nobody's rung them. Miss Dearing certainly hadn't, yet there was only me and her in the house.'

For a moment both girls were silent. Ella wondered if Nancy's fears were getting the better of her.

'That's not all. There was a head that fell off the wall, just like that!'

'A *head*?'

'I'll show you.'

Nancy led Ella out of the kitchen and down the

hallway. She rolled her eyes and Ella looked up. In the gloomy shadows of the hall a vast selection of exotic wildlife stared down.

'There's no gap now.'

'Someone stuck it back up.'

'Which one was it?'

Nancy pointed to the stuffed head of a wild boar. One of its cheeks bulged and the tusk on the other side was a bit wonky. 'Was it always that shape?' she asked, thinking of the anteater at the museum.

Nancy shook her head in scorn. 'Never looked at it closely before, not 'til I fell over it in the dark!'

Ella reached into her blazer pocket and pulled out a notebook, followed by a stubby, chewed-looking pencil, and scribbled away. 'We must be scientific,' she said, 'right from the start.' She counted the animals' heads, as if this was important, and calculated the position of the wild boar—bottom row, six along and three from the end. You never knew what was going to matter in an investigation so you had to take everything into consideration. She had learned that from Nancy last summer.

'The next step is that you must show me where all the other spooky—er, unexplained—events took place. I want a guided tour.'

'The next step is for me to get those scones out of the oven before they burn!' said Nancy. 'You might've got a half-holiday, but I haven't.'

'Listen, though,' Ella hissed as they went back to the

kitchen. 'I thought it would be useful to know more about the background of this house, if we're going to—'

But there was Miss Dearing lifting the lid of a cold teapot and peering inside. 'Ella, dear! How lovely to see you.'

Ella raised her eyebrows at Nancy, who gave the faintest shake of her head; meaning that Miss Dearing knew nothing of the real reason for the visit.

Ella was on her best behaviour while the scones came out of the oven, the kettle was boiled, and a plate of sandwiches appeared from the pantry. She sat at the table and answered Miss Dearing's questions about school as patiently as she could. No, it had not improved. Yes, she had been in further trouble. Today was Founder's Day, which meant a boring assembly about the school's history and then a stupid hockey match between Upper and Lower School teams, but now she was free. Yes, she would love to see the new donkeys, but first Nancy was going to show her the wonders of the Grange.

They left Miss Dearing to her second cup of tea and escaped.

Nancy began with the Drawing Room. 'This is where Miss Dearing was when she swore she had not rung the bell—and here is the bell-pull.' Ella immediately reached for the tasselled brocade and pulled. 'You won't hear it in here,' Nancy said, 'only outside the kitchen. Miss Dearing'll wonder what's going on.'

Ella made another note. She looked down and saw that she was standing on a zebra skin. She looked up and saw the hides of yet more animals stretched out around the walls.

'Um . . . what does Miss Dearing think of the decorations? Given that she would rather usher a fly out of the window than squash it with a rolled-up newspaper, like most people.'

Ella gazed about at shields, and spears, and daunting masks. Glass-fronted cabinets displayed odd, fierce-looking ornaments. Hardly the most restful things to have surrounding you in an English Drawing Room; she wondered where they came from and who they belonged to originally. Her own house was full of strange and curious objects but it was nothing compared to this.

'I think the decorations are the last thing on her mind,' Nancy mused. 'She's been so taken up with where to put her animals, and the vegetable garden, and the washing line. Then she's learning to drive a motor car—and—and someone's sending her nasty letters!'

'No! Who?'

Nancy grimaced. 'They're not signed.'

'How do you know? Did she tell you?'

Nancy's grimace stretched even further. She glanced away. Ella caught her eye. 'You sneaked a look, didn't you? Did she leave them lying around?'

'No. I saw her burn one, but I got the impression it wasn't the first. The next one I—er—intercepted.'

Ella tried to sound as calm and neutral as possible, but she was tremendously excited. 'Have you still got it? As evidence?' She scrabbled to open her notebook again. 'Nancy, you know what this is, don't you? It's a real, *proper* mystery again.'

29. LOGICAL EXPLANATION NO. 1

The Library, a double-length room filled floor-to-ceiling with specially-built bookshelves, had Ella's eyes popping in awe.

'Father would adore all this,' she told Nancy, and reached out cautiously to touch a book. It was so ancient that the binding resembled flaky pastry, and threatened to crumble away. She moved down the room. On closer inspection, the books proved as dull as ditchwater. There were endless bound copies of old magazines, sets of law books, Minutes of the Society of this and that. Rows of three-volume Victorian novels that looked as if they'd never been opened.

Ella thought of Seabourne Public Library and how small and shabby it was in comparison.

'I've been conducting some research into Oxcoombe Grange,' she said, skipping over the help Professor Goring had given her. 'I found out that there used to be a priory here. Did you ever learn about Henry VIII at your school? Well, he needed money very badly. He disbanded all the monasteries and priories—the richest ones first—so that he could take their lands, and houses, and gold plate, and jewels.'

'Why did monks need jewels?' asked Nancy, but Ella ignored this and hurried on.

'Then it became the property of Sir William de Warne, one of Henry's supporters. It belonged to his family for hundreds of years. They must have let it become very run-down and neglected because I found an old engraving of it covered in ivy, with holes in the roof. Artists used to go round drawing picturesque ruins like that—it was very fashionable for a while. Next the Grange was sold and the new owner spent a lot of money on it. He enlarged the old house and turned the fields where sheep grazed into gardens.'

'Miss Dearing told me that bit,' Nancy said. 'Mr Duggan's grandad, I think it was. I don't see what this has got to do with—'

'Here comes the good part,' Ella interrupted. 'The de Warnes never lived here much. They rented out the land and let the village get by without any help from the lord of the manor. Or any *interference*. And Oxcoombe Bay became known for smuggling! The church here was nicknamed "the Smugglers' Church"—I saw a sketch of it called that. Perhaps the villagers couldn't scrape a living any other way. Or perhaps they enjoyed breaking the law, cheating the taxman—and the money they made. I even found an old map. It's in my satchel under the kitchen table.'

Nancy led the way out of the Library by the far door.

Ella lowered her voice in case Miss Dearing was anywhere nearby. 'Then this new lord of the manor came along, determined to live on the spot and make everything neat and tidy—imagine that! I can't think the smugglers liked it one bit. But later on Miss Dearing's godfather inherited the house. Since he was always away on his travels that would suit the village fine—'

'And now Miss Dearing's come and looks like settling in . . .' Nancy added.

'Exactly!' They were heading towards the stairs. Ella pulled at a door handle opposite, saying, 'Wait. What's in here? You haven't shown me this room yet.'

'We're going to look at the Japanese warrior. There's nothing much in there but—'

'But stuff!' said Ella, as the door swung open. A wall of *stuff* greeted her: more of Mr Duggan's vast collection, not arranged around the room as decoration but all crammed in together with just narrow passages between, like a mad museum.

'Miss Dearing says her godfather brought back so many things he didn't even know what he had,' Nancy continued. 'I believe the attics are full as well.'

'Good heavens!' said Ella, and pulled the door sharply shut on the chaos.

Something heavy thudded to the floor. Ella jumped back, knocking into Nancy, who let out a small scream.

The something on the floor had a long pointed nose

and sharp curlicue horns. 'Good heavens . . .' Ella said again, under her breath this time. She reached out to touch its moth-eaten nose. 'Poor thing.'

'*Poor thing*? It could have killed you!'

'Or you.'

Nancy was staring upwards. 'It was right next to the pig's head.'

'And all it took was someone shutting this door too hard. There, I think, we have—Logical Explanation No. 1.'

Ella grinned.

Nancy did not grin back. 'Only problem is,' she said, 'who was it shut the door?'

30. OGSCOME

NANCY'S JOURNAL

Ella was here & I gave her the Grand Tour. She seemed to think she'd solved one Mystery—the pig's head—yet it only <u>raised another</u>. How did a door slam all by itself? But she was pleased as punch & said it was a very good start. I told her '<u>You</u> don't have to live here!' I may have raised my voice at that point.

I thoght of Ella's house—with Prof. Otter always in his study & Mrs Prebble always in the kitchen & nothing being too huge or too dark or too far away—or anything like 400 years old. (Even if Mr Duggan kicked the bucket in Switzer-land—just think how many others must have lived & DIED here in that time.)

Then she got another one of those gleams in her eye. She dragged her satchel from under the table & opened it. 'Look—here's what I found in Seabourne Libary.' She took out a crumpled old bit of paper that looked like it had fallen in a sink full of water & been dried out (badly).

It was A MAP.

She said she was not supposed to have it at all cos it had come from the Refference Libary where all the rare stuff was kept & no one was meant to take it out. Ella said 'Miss Valentine would have my GUTS FOR GARTERS if she knew!' (She said it in a thrilled tone tho.)

The map seemed so <u>delicate</u> I was scared to touch it. Ella pointed to something right in the middle. 'See here. This is where we are now.'

I could not make head or tail of it. I will try & draw it here:

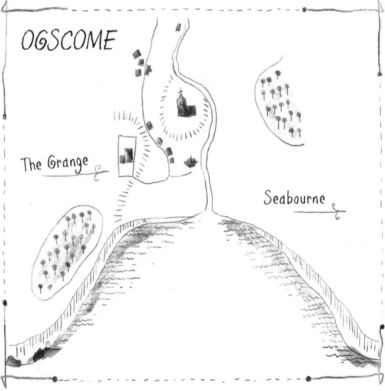

I ponted out there's no forest here & no big river. 'There isn't NOW,' Ella said (snapped, more like). 'This map was drawn hundreds of years ago when it was all different. See this?'

A word—the letters so bent and squashed it was hard to read. Then the penny dropped:

OGSCOME

That was how they spelled it hundreds of years ago.

That's when the map sort of <u>changed before my eyes</u> & began to make sense. There was no bridge & no road up the steep hill back to Seabourne & not so many houses but I could see that the village & the lane & the sea were in the right places. That cross is where the church stands. They've even drawn the mound around it. Also there is a stream here—the one that goes past the Mill & under the bridge—even if it's only small & gets lost in the fields either side. By the river there was a mark like a tiny boat.

Ella said 'Now look here. It's a different shape but this must be Oxcoombe Grange.' It didn't look anything like as big & the line that showed the shape of the garden was all wrong. But it was in the right spot. I suppose if you knocked down the 100-year-old NEW half it would fit.

Ella went on 'But this is the best part of all and I'm sure it's to do with the smugglers.' She ran her finger round the bay to the cliffs under the headland & some funny black marks. I couldn't make them out at all until she said 'CAVES!'

Which was the moment Miss Dearing strode in. In a flash Ella put her school hat over the map. Miss D. did not appear to notice for she said 'Are you ready Ella? Peg & I are off to see a man about a donkey & if you like we can drop you at Oxcoombe station on our way.'

Ella did promise to come back on Saturday & kept winking & pulling faces as she was hurried out the door. So that was that. It leaves me with more questions than answers.

The door shut behind Ella & Miss Dearing & the house fell silent & still. VERY silent & still. As if it was just waiting for them to go.

WHAT I WANT TO KNOW NOW:-

1. Who—or what—shut that door & made the pig's head fall down?
2. If it was a WHO—what were they up to?
3. If it was a WHAT—is it <u>sad Monks</u> or <u>angry Smugglers</u> or <u>old dead folk</u> in Mr Duggan or William Dewarn's family that haunt this place?
4. Or is it someone we haven't even thoght of yet?
5. Is the village still angry with whoever lives at the Grange?
6. Is that why someone hates Miss Dearing so bad they send her letters saying she is a DISGRACE?
7. Will I be able to keep Miss Dearing from <u>further worry</u>?
8. When will I get a decent night's sleep?

<u>People to speak to next:—</u>

Mrs Lubbock
Mr Oakapple (nobody ever talks to him)

129

31. STANDOFFISH

As the cart pulled out of the yard, a fine rain began to fall and Ella was forced to put her hated hat back on. She wondered if it was *letting down the school* to be seen in uniform while bowling along in a cart painted like a garish fairground ride. In fact there was no one to see her. The clatter of Pancho's hooves cut through the stillness of Oxcoombe village at mid-afternoon.

'Don't you find this a bit dreary after Seabourne?' she remarked to Miss Dearing, who sat beside her in a crackling brown mackintosh and a wide black hat.

'It certainly isn't as sociable as The Green. Or as lively as Seabourne. But then I wouldn't expect that.'

'Did you know it was unfriendly before you moved here?' Ella didn't bother to lower her voice. If Oxcoombe was being standoffish, it should hear the truth.

'I visited my godfather only every year or so. There'd be a huge fire burning in the Drawing Room, a delicious tea laid on, and we talked of world affairs, just the two of us. Then his carriage, or later his car, would drive me home.' Miss Dearing sighed. 'He didn't really mix with the village. As I've told Nancy, my godfather preferred his own company. I think he was very shy.'

Ella was genuinely perplexed. 'How does a shy man travel the world?'

'Perhaps it's easier if everyone is a stranger, speaking a strange language . . .'

Ella tried a new tack. 'The Grange is very large—and old—compared to Apple Cottage.'

'Apple Cottage is rather old itself!' Miss Dearing chuckled.

Would she really be laughing if she found her new home at all creepy? Ella wondered. This cart-ride was the perfect opportunity for interrogation yet she was getting nowhere! She pressed on: 'Both houses have seen a great deal of history. Are there any stories—about, well—about Oxcoombe Grange's strange past?'

Miss Dearing murmured, 'Some people seem to think it rather strange now.'

Ella gritted her teeth. 'Um, what will you do with Mr Duggan's collections?'

This time it was a while before Miss Dearing replied. Pancho's hooves tapped gently on, the harness rattled, the wheels ground over the badly-made road. Peg sat very upright in her man's oilskin jacket. It was as if everyone was listening for the answer.

'You know, I really hadn't thought.'

'*I* have,' said Ella. 'Because it seems odd, Miss Dearing, for someone like you who is so very fond of animals—real live ones—to keep so many nasty old bits of *dead* ones around you.'

Silence. They passed the signpost that pointed towards the station. Peg flicked the reins to make Pancho trot faster.

'You should sell them, or give them to the museum,' Ella said. 'You could get someone who knows about such things to come and look them over. I mean, I'm not sure if anyone would want to buy a moth-eaten antelope head, but there must be *some* stuff of value.' She remembered the horse statue that so fascinated Professor Goring and her father. 'There are definitely things that people would pay good money for.'

They rounded a corner and there was the station. Ella jumped down, thanked Miss Dearing, and waved goodbye to Peg. But the girl didn't notice. She was staring at nothing, with a distracted look on her face.

'Oh dear,' thought Ella. 'I've said rude things about the place she was born in. Where the Shantos have lived for generations. She'll probably go home and tell them all how snooty and stuck-up Miss Dearing's visitors are. I've just made everything worse.'

32. MOST TALKATIVE

NANCY'S JOURNAL

After Ella & Miss Dearing left I wanted to get out of the house so I took a walk along to the Mill. But it was all dead quiet & there was a sign on the bakehouse door saying CLOSED. I don't know if Mrs Lubbock was out or having a snooze—I <u>do</u> know that she gets up very early every day to make the bread. It's hard to talk to her for she's always so busy. Came back past the village shop—also closed. Seems like it always is. Miss D. has fixed for a grocer from Seabourne to deliver & now my pantry shelves are full & <u>almost</u> perfectly organized.

I decided to try Mr Oakapple next. I took him out some tea & a bun so he'd have to stop clipping or mowing or whatever he was doing. Turns out he was sweeping leaves ready for a Bonfire. I didn't know how to start so asked him about the garden—he turned out <u>most talkative</u> on that subject. As if he was just longing to tell somebody how it was all so much better under Mr Duggan.

What I discovered (leaving out a load of stuff about gardens) is:—

-He has worked here since he was a boy.

- The old Head Gardener back in Mr Duggan's father's time took him on & trained him.

-Before the War he had an Under-Gardener to help.

-The Under-Gardener was EDWARD SHANTO!

'He was coming along all right he was,' said Mr Oak & we both stood silent for a bit thinking how the War had mucked up such a lot of things. Then—hoping what I was going to say wouldn't make him cross—I asked 'What about taking on Spud or Ears? Train them up in his place?'

All he did was shake his head. 'You could trust Edward.'

Edward was the one Peg liked too.

Then Mr Oak said the Shantos are best suited to water—not land. Always had been. Their dad was a fisherman before his boat went down & him with it. They've still got a little row-boat but it's not enough for much of a catch. Long ago—before there was a bridge in Oxcoombe—Shantos ran a ferry across the river for folk who needed it. Made their living that way. 'River Ox was wide enough & deep enough for boats to go up & down it then' he said 'til THEM IN CHARGE let the river choke up & slow down.' He tipped his head towards the house when he said that. So I asked when was this? He didn't know. His grandad's grandad's time maybe.

It began to rain hard so we couldn't go on chatting. Mr Oak headed for his tool-shed & I went back indoors to write this down. Seems wherever you look about this place, a Shanto is mixed up in it.

33. APPARITION

NANCY'S JOURNAL

Woke in the dim grey dawn to find an ~~Apper~~ Apparishun leaning over my bed! An olden-times lady in a long frock. My heart nearly BURST!!

'Nancy! You've overslept. The range has gone out & the kitchen is freezing.'

A ghost wouldn't say that. (A ghost wouldn't talk at all.)

A ghost wouldn't follow it with 'Sorry if I startled you.' (<u>Would</u> it?)

I had the covers pulled up to my nose. I may have let out a bit of a screech too.

Miss Dearing looked appolergetic. But with that lace cap on her head, hair all loose & a long grey dressing gown on, it was easy to mistake her for someone from long ago.

I dashed cold water on my face, got dressed & ran downstairs. The kitchen felt cold as a grave & as silent. No strange noises—and none to report in the last few days. Maybe all the work, inside & out, has scared it (them?) off. I got the Excelsior going & by the time it was warm enough to heat a kettle I'd stopped shivering enough to write this down. (Still a bit wobbly from Miss Dearing's ghostly appearance tho.)

So that's another Logical Explanation. Miss Dearing walks about at night dressed like a ghost.

34. GIRLS & EDUCATION

NANCY'S JOURNAL

<u>Today after lunch</u>

—all alone in the kitchen again

—I heard a whole lot of bumping and dragging

— longer & louder than ever before!

This time I was sure where it was: in the passageway just outside. My heart was in my mouth. But COME WHAT MAY I was going to catch it, so I threw open the door . . .

What did I find but Peg & Miss Dearing struggling with a fat sofa & a narrow doorway? Once they wiggled it thru they both looked up at me & grinned. Like they expected me to burst out clapping! My knees were shaking & all I wanted to do was collapse on that sofa myself.

Miss Dearing dusted off her hands & announced 'From now on I shall only use the formal rooms when I have visitors. It is quite DISMAL sitting there on my own. This will be much more practical & far less work for you Nancy.'

(She isn't changing her bedroom tho. Still got to traipse along there 10 times a day!)

The room she means to use is v. modest—with a fine view of the tool-shed & the backyard pump. I think in days gone by it may have been the Housekeeper's Sitting

Room. There's a neat little fireplace with a hook for a tea kettle & another with a toasting fork hanging from it. Miss Dearing & Peg went on pushing furniture about & fetching in more bits & bobs—until Miss D. stood back & said 'There! Very snug.'

Which is what she calls it now: The Snuggery.

I lugged in a bucket of coal for the fire & Miss Dearing sank down in her old armchair from Apple Cottage saying 'Splendid!' (Oh if only every hour at Oxcoombe Grange could be as ordinary & carefree as this!)

But barely had my employer sat down than she jumped up again. 'I'm forgetting myself. Nancy—we must be off!' I asked what new chore she had in mind. Turns out it was tidying ourselves up to go & attend A LECTURE (posh word for a Talk) in Seabourne. I fear I said 'What—me?' in a v. impertinent tone & one which would have Lady Pouncey sack me on the spot.

I did wunder if all the heaving about of furniture had made Miss D. feel a bit dizzy. But she was quite clear in the head. In fact she was on Fine Form today—quite her old self. (Glad I kept that nasty letter away from her.) She said 'The lecture is to be on GIRLS & EDUCATION and will give you lots to think about. You may not wish to stay in Service all your life.' As if I wanted to go into Service in the first place!

But I've had my fill of Education thanks very much. At Main Road School they moved me up to the top class when I was 11—which meant I had to do the same lessons over & over again until I turned 14 & was able to leave. Just thinking about the sound of squeeky chalk on a blackboard gives me a stummick ache.

Then—supprise supprise!—the Lecture was not half as bad as I ~~ants~~ antissipated. It was all about the jobs young women could be trained to do: being meckanics & drivers (just like Alfred) or gardeners (like Mr Oakapple) or raising animals & running farms. There were 3 ladies who spoke & another who announced their names and stopped them if they went on too long. Then there were questions at the end & anyone could put their hand up & ask something. (Not me. No fear.) Someone stood up & said 'Were these jobs for women cos they could not be wives & mothers any more what with all the men lost in the War?' Then someone else shouted—without putting up their hand—that it was men needed the jobs, not young ladies. I wish Aunty Bee could have been there! She'd have something to say about that.

Of course not a word about training to be a Detective—or how to get into films. (I should have put my hand up & asked about that.) I know some folk think acting & singing is not a respecktable job for a Young Lady—but now it seems that SWINGING BUCKETS OF PIGSWILL ABOUT is!! No one ever thinks about girls becoming Detectives at all. They see it only as a job for grown men with mustaches & shady-looking hats.

35. DONKEYS OUT!

NANCY'S JOURNAL

Right old carry-on today. First I knew of it was Peg banging on the kitchen window, shouting 'Donkeys out!' Miss Dearing came dashing from the Snuggery in her house slippers. Suddenly we were all 3 running about outside like mad chickens.

'How many got out?' Miss Dearing wanted to know & I wanted to know what in flaming heavens I was supposed to do if I found one! 3 little donkeys down on the Bowling Green were standing quite calm in their pen—but their heads were all facing one way & they looked like they knew something. What they knew was that the Crokay Lawn pen had given way & the donkeys in that had bust out.

Miss D. shouted 'Get help! Where are Spud & Ears?' Peg shook her head—her brothers weren't working here today. 'Where's Mr Oakapple?' I could see him far off tending a smoky Bonfire. No help from that quarter. Nor from the sneaky faces that appeared at a few lace curtains—I expect our naybours in the village were enjoying a glimpse of us running about like fools.

I must say it's supprising what LOOKS LIKE A DONKEY when you're LOOKING FOR A DONKEY—& then turns out to be something else. A bit of grey stone wall. A pile of

something round the side of a cottage. Rocks on the beach.
Cos that's where we headed once Peg's shouts reached us.
She was running over the shingle with her boots sort of
SQUUMPING and her coat flapping like a great big kite. If
I was a donkey & seen that site come crashing towards me
I'd have stampeeded. Which is almost what they did.

They were down on a sandy stretch and when they
turned & looked at Peg they kicked up their heels & took
off. Just like it was fun. I think it was Gilda leading
the way.

I didn't go as far as the wet sand—not in my only
decent pair of shoes. Miss Dearing didn't hold back tho &
hurried down there with her buttercup-yellow shawl flying
behind. The donkeys had stopped all their GIDDY GADDING
ABOUT & stood with their noses towards the sea & their
feet not quite in it. Just like the summer Day Trippers!!

But they made a big mistake. When the tide's halfway
that beach goes in and out—small bays with great rocks
between. They'd reached a tiny bay hemmed in on the far
side by rocky crags. They were stuck. Nowhere to turn
but the sea or the way they'd come & that was blocked by
Peg—moving all slow & calm—her arms out wide. She was
all right with her rubber boots on but Miss Dearing (I had
to admire her pluck!) pulled off her slippers, stuffed them
into her pockets, & splashed right after her. Peg had ropes

& halters with her & it wasn't long before they were all tied up & safe.

So that was how we paraded back up the lane: me & Miss Dearing leading 2 donkeys a-piece. Peg had 3. I said 'The circus has come to town,' but I said it under my breath cos Miss Dearing—up front with Gilda and Pancho—looked perfectly happy again. Nor did I want Peg (bringing up the rear in case of any trouble) to hear me. There were more curtains lifted & one lady just happened to be going out her gate & another busy with her washing line tho she had no washing with her. Miss Dearing called out a cheerful 'Good morning!' & they bid her Good morning in return. They <u>had to</u>. She was so nice and frendly they could hardly turn their backs.

The donkeys couldn't be put in their broken pen so we tied them up in the yard & the littlest one in the garage. I was going to make us tea but Miss Dearing said she needed something stronger—which only turned out to be <u>coffee</u>. Not a Drop of Medicinal Brandy which is what my Gran takes after a NASTY SHOCK.

We sat down in the Snuggery. Peg clutched her cup & looked at the floor. 'Donkeys wouldn't have never got out if Ears & Spud had done <u>a proper job</u>' she muttered.

I think Miss Dearing wanted to make her feel it wasn't such a disaster. 'Oh come now Peg. I think it was more like Gilda's fault. One small crack in the rail was all it needed. She's a very forceful carrickter. That fence can be mended easy enough.' But Peg kept shaking her head—going 'Just can't trust 'em.'

Which is pretty much what Mr Oakapple said.

ODD OCKURRENCES AT OXCOOMBE GRANGE (CONTINUED)

Latest events:—

9. Mysterious ringing of Drawing Room bell! Still un-explained.

10. Pig's head fell off wall of its own accord!!
LOGICAL EXPLANATION: Shutting nearby door (hard) makes heads fall down.
Proved & witnessed by Ella Otter.

11. (At least 2) Anonymouse letters sent to Miss D. Delivered by hand.
Who by? Someone who wants her to GO BACK TO THE HOVEL WHERE SHE BELONGS.

12. Ghost of a lady in olden-day dress appeared.
Where: In my bedroom.
When: At dawn.
LOGICAL EXPLANATION: Turned out to be Miss D. in night clothes & poor light.

13. Dragging & bumping noises.
Where: Downstairs hallway.
When: Afternoon.
LOGICAL EXPLANATION: Turned out to be Miss D. &
Peg shifting furniture.

14. Donkeys pushed down fence & escaped. Just an
accident? Peg blames her brothers for not making
fence stronger. Miss D. blames donkeys. Could it be
someone else? The letter-writer??

Ella is coming tomorrow. If I show her this list I fear she
will laugh at me!!

36. DANGEROUS DRIVING

Unfortunately for Ella, Professor Otter never gave rewards. Nor did he stoop to bribes. He felt that *achievement* should be reward enough. Therefore no treats followed when Ella passed the entrance exam to the Grammar School with top marks, nor in September when she began her first term ever at an actual school. But a few weeks later—and nowhere near her birthday—a rather wonderful bicycle stood in the hall of their house (the only time it *would* stand in the hall, as ever afterwards its tyres were plastered with mud). It was glossy green and the perfect height for Ella. There was a bell, and a basket, and a battery-powered lamp clipped to the handlebars.

'Now you can be even more independent,' her father said.

Ella beamed. 'Can I ride it to school?'

'It would take you all morning to get there, and all afternoon to get back.'

No bad thing, thought Ella.

'But when it isn't a school day—' the professor began.

'Which is hardly ever!'

'Which is two-sevenths of the week,' her father went

calmly on, 'your bicycle will allow you great freedom. As well as in the school holidays, and come the longer evenings of the spring—'

'Which is a million years away!'

'Which is, as you know, six months away—'

'*Six months!*'

'You will be able to get out and about a great deal.'

'Yes, Father. Thank you, Father.'

'I hope that's not mockery I can hear in your voice, Ella.'

'It isn't, Father. Truly. My voice just comes out that way. It isn't something I can help.'

Her father raised one eyebrow, a skill Ella had practised in vain. Trying to keep a straight face, she said, 'I hope that isn't a mocking eyebrow, Father?'

'It's a fatherly eyebrow, Ella,' her father said in his soft American accent.

They looked at each other and smiled. The reward which wasn't a reward had been a great success.

On Saturday Ella wheeled the bike, now much less shiny and new, out of the garden gate. Sausage perched in the wicker basket at the front. He wore an eager expression, and a red woollen jumper to keep out the cold. Mrs Prebble had knitted it for him, making up the pattern as she went along. She left holes for his two front legs, and added a polo neck. Everyone, including Sausage, thought he looked very smart.

Ella headed for Oxcoombe. She knew that the hill leading down to it was steeper than any she had ridden down so far but the bicycle had excellent brakes.

'Hang on, Sausage,' she yelled.

Sausage put his noble nose into the wind. His soft ears flapped behind his head. Ella gently squeezed the brakes as she felt the wheels spin faster. The cottages of Oxcoombe, the church and the Grange, were just toy-town buildings below them, not at all dissimilar to the map she'd shown Nancy. But they were getting bigger—and closer—all the time.

A sudden rush of wind, a roar, and a dark red car flashed past her. Ella wobbled in a wide arc, saw the roadside ditch veer close, and wrestled with the handlebars. Poor Sausage had crouched low in his basket, his nose hidden in his old blanket from home, and his ears flat to his head. Are we going over, are we? Ella thought. And then, with another giant swerve, her front wheel was heading fast down the centre of the road again.

'What an excellent, strong, reliable, bike this is,' she muttered. 'I must tell Father.' But then she thought that he wouldn't really like to hear how near she and Sausage had come to a gruesome end in the ditch. And all because of a very dangerous driver. Ella knew exactly who that driver was.

Ahead, the Daimler slowed down and swung off the lane. Ella swooped past and saw that it had turned into the drive of a house, a big ugly white house set halfway down the hill. So *that* was where Juniper Vale lived.

37. CANINE POWERS

NANCY'S JOURNAL

Ella turned up today with a bright red face & that dog of hers in a bright red jumper. She said 'I came all the way here on my bycycle. We were nearly killed by that wicked Mrs Vale. Weren't we Sausage?'

Sausage didn't look like he had suffered any damidge. He looked like he was ENJOYING the adventure.

'We've come to test for Super-natural Ockurrences' she announced. 'Sausage is going to apply his Canine Powers in all the places around the house where strange events have been observed. Dogs are very sensitive. If the Grange <u>has</u> got anything beyond our skills to detect—then Sausage will show us.' She must have seen the look on my face cos she explained 'It's just to make my experiment more sientifick. I have to TEST MY THEORY.'

'What <u>is</u> your theory?'

'You <u>know</u> what it is!! That there's a logical reason for everything you've seen & heard. You don't have to be all jumpy & scared of every bump & rattle you hear.'

My face must have done something else then cos she muttered 'Sorry.'

<u>According to Ella there may be a super-natural presence if a dog does any of the following:—</u>
* whines
* growls
* flattens ears
* fur stands on end
* stares at fixed spot where nothing is to be seen
* slinks away with its belly on the ground
* or just runs in terror.

What it will <u>not do</u> is act like an ordinary everyday dog. (Tho in my experiense dogs often growl & whine for no other reason than they are growly whiney types.)

Next Ella asked 'Is Miss Dearing in? Does she know what we are up to?'

Of course she doesn't. I'm not so stupid as to let my Employer know that I will be messing about TESTING FOR SPOOKS when I am meant to be washing dishes or laying fires or 100 other household tasks. I told Ella that she's gone off with Peg to fetch another poor donkey that needs rescuing.

'Then we have the freedom of the house!'

She put Sausage down on the kitchen floor to explore. No bad signs from him at all—except when the Excelsior gave out one of its loud clangs. I said 'There—that's what it does—for no reason that I can see.'

'You may have heard many strange noises in the kitchen Nancy. But our trusty hound tells us there is nothing untoward here.'

Nothing here <u>now</u> I said to myself.

Sausage made a dash for the door so Ella followed shouting 'Hallway' as if she was in charge. He went along sniffing at everything. He found it v. interesting but in an ordinary doggy way. Near the front door there is a horrible grey leathery stump full of walking sticks & umbrellas. Miss

Dearing told me it is an Elephant's Foot. That got top marks from Sausage!

Ella took out her notebook & wrote something down. I said that Elephant's nothing to do with his Ghost-sniffing Powers but she said she had to note everything that happened.

We tried him next in the Dining Room, Drawing Room & Libary. I think he would have stayed all day sniffing at the zebra skin rug on the Drawing Room floor if Ella had not pulled him away. Sausage did not think much of the Libary. Just as we walked in, the wind bashed hard at the big windows & he cowered. Ella asked 'Is it always this chilly? Are some places colder than others? They say that's a sign.' I said it was cold cos it was twice the size of the other rooms—with leaky windows that catch all the sea breezes as Miss Dearing calls them. I call them GALES.

Ella made more notes.

'Hmmm . . .' Ella went on as if she was thinking out loud. I know that look on her face—I've seen it before—when she's working on a Theory & her mind is racing. 'Mr Duggan spent his life travelling and collecting. He kept his treasures here, in the house he was born in—and died in. Did he die here? I wonder in which room?'

'In Switzer-land as a matter of fact.' I was pleased I could answer that one.

'Now his god-daughter lives here. She cares nothing for old masks & animal skins—only for the happiness of living creatures. Do you think the UN-QUIET SPIRIT OF DOMINIC DUGGAN haunts this house?!'

That's all I need—for Ella to get spooked! We both shivered like icycles in an east wind & Sausage whined to be let out of the libary door.

So far that's:—
*whining
*cowering
*running away

There was still upstairs to try. Even Ella went slowly for once. She put her foot on the first step & said 'Those flitting shapes you've seen—there's a reason for that you know'—tho to my mind her voice sounded bit hollow. She went on 'Father told me that humans see best at the edge of their eyes when it's getting dark. So when you turn to look right at the shape you won't see anything—because you're looking with a different part of your eye. The part that sees best in light.'

It sounded good but—what about the shape itself? That doesn't prove there's nothing there. Just that I won't see it by looking straight. She didn't say anything to that!

GRRRRR!

The Japanese Worrier loomed above us all <u>shadowy</u> & grim. Sausage was twisting about in her grasp. She put him down at the Worrier's feet—but he was back in her arms again before you could say Jack Robinson! Lips drawn up so his teeth showed & growling in his throat. There's something about that Worrier the dog didn't like—didn't like at all. (Me too.)

There's something about upstairs he didn't like neither, when Ella tried to take him further on. He struggled & struggled then jumped down & ran away.

I looked at Ella. She looked back at me. The Canine Powers were working ALL TOO WELL.

38. DOWN BELOW

Ella tucked her notebook back in her skirt pocket and followed Sausage down the stairs. She was still determined to be *systematic* and *scientific*. There was one more item to check—the servants' bells. Nancy showed her where they were, in the passageway just outside the kitchen. Sausage had to be held up to sniff each bell. He was quite calm again now, but showed absolutely no interest and wriggled to be put down. As soon as he was on the floor he trotted off and scrabbled at a nearby door.

'What's in there?'

'Just a cupboard.'

'Can I look?'

Nancy shrugged. She didn't go through her bunch of keys. 'Nothing worth locking the door for,' she said. The cupboard was dark. Taking up most of the space was a tall tea-chest. She pulled out a handful of dusty, empty sacks to show Ella, who passed them down to Sausage to sniff.

Ella leaned over the tea-chest and craned her neck. 'What's that?' She pointed to the roof of the cupboard. It looked like the underside of a narrow, twisting wooden staircase. '*Secret* stairs?'

'No, just the back stairs. You know, the ones that servants use.'

'Where do the other steps lead to?'

'What other steps?'

'The ones Sausage has just run down!'

Sausage had squeezed around the side of the tea-chest and disappeared into the dark.

'What?' Nancy shrieked. She stuck her head into the cupboard, nudging Ella out of the way. 'I've been looking for a cellar—and the way in—for ages.' When she pulled her head out again, her eyes were bright and her cheeks pink with excitement.

'Lady Pouncey *said* there ought to be a cellar. For the wine. It must be cool and dark and spacious, she says.'

'Who on earth is Lady Pouncey?'

But Nancy was too busy dragging at the tea-chest to answer. Ella tried to help. Suddenly it came free with a jerk. Nancy slipped backwards and flung out her arms to save herself. On the wall behind her, several bells jangled.

'Logical Explanation No. 2,' Ella remarked coolly.

Nancy didn't seem to hear. 'Just fetching something,' she said, and scampered away. Ella heard pounding up the wooden stairs inside the cupboard, then down again. Nancy reappeared, waving a battery torch.

Ella made some rapid notes and when she looked up again she was alone in the passageway.

'Nancy?'

'Down here . . .'

Ella squeezed past the tea-chest and into the cupboard,

following the muffled sounds and the wavering torchlight. The steps beneath her feet were stone. The air grew colder and smelled of earth. She reached out to steady herself and felt clammy brick walls. Creeping on round a curve in the stairs, she bumped right into Nancy's back. The torch-beam swung about, lighting up vaulted ceilings, dingy archways, cobwebs so ancient they hung in ropes and curtains.

'The cellar . . .' Nancy whispered in awe. 'Must run right under the kitchen.'

'Right under the house, I'd say,' breathed Ella. She clutched at Nancy's arm. 'Where did Sausage go?'

Nancy played the torch low across the floor. It gleamed fainter and fainter and still didn't reach the end of the darkness.

Ella began to whistle. It sounded very eerie in the echoing spaces of the cellar.

'I wonder what that whistling sounds like from upstairs?' Nancy murmured. 'I wonder what this sounds like?' She stamped her foot on the floor, but the floor was stone, covered in dirt, and made no sound at all.

Ella grabbed the torch from her. 'We must find Sausage! I can't lose him. What will Father say?'

She began walking forward slowly and felt Nancy clutch at the back of her jumper. They both called the dog's name, in low cautious voices. Cautious of what, Ella could not have said.

'Look, there's a chink of light.'

On the far side a tiny, filthy pane of glass at the top of an archway let in a dim grey shine. Ella shone the torch below it. 'I think there was a bigger window there, but it's been bricked up.' They crept on to the next archway and found the same thing. 'You know what this means? Once upon a time this part of the house wasn't so far below ground. It must have sunk—or they built up the ground around it. We're in the most ancient part of Oxcoombe Grange. Think of all the—.'

Ella halted. Up ahead she could hear something. Scraping and scratching. It stopped for a heartbeat, then started again.

'*Rats?*' hissed Nancy.

'Very *big* rats,' Ella whispered back. She pointed the torch and at last its faint light picked out a creature. It was Sausage, ignoring the girls in his fever to scratch at the base of a door.

'Keys, Nancy,' Ella demanded, but Nancy was already working her way through the bunch of keys, large and small, discounting those which she knew opened something else. There were three big iron ones she had yet to try. As Ella held the torch steady she put each to the heavy old lock on the door. Not one of them fitted.

Nancy shivered. 'We ought to get out of here. Miss Dearing'll be back soon. Might be up there, even now, wondering where I am.'

Ella bent to pick up the little dog, then stopped. She shone the torch beam on the ground. 'Well, look at that!'

The light picked out a footprint in the dust and dirt. Ella set her shoe beside it carefully. The print was of a man's boot, large and perfect and new.

ODD OCKURRENCES AT OXCOOMBE GRANGE (CONTINUED)

Latest events:—

9. Mysterious ringing of Drawing Room bell! — ~~Still un-explained~~.
LOGICAL EXPLANATION: Hit it when falling over, dragging a box that blocked entrance to cellar steps. (Something to do with No. 10 below???)

10. Pig's head fell off wall of its own accord!!
LOGICAL EXPLANATION: Shutting nearby door (hard) makes heads fall down. Proved & witnessed by Ella Otter.

39. EVEN SPOOKIER

NANCY'S JOURNAL

Expected another Sleepless Night after all our discoveries but in fact I nodded off right away. Fell deep asleep. Then suddenly I was WIDE AWAKE again! <u>Something</u> must have woke me. I sat up—my eyes & ears out on stalks again. After a bit I even got out of bed & went to the stairs and listened. (When you <u>listen very hard</u> your ears sort of swish of their own accord & you can't hear anything over that.) Next I crept down the back stairs & pushed the kitchen door open <u>very very slowly</u>. Nothing there.

I thoght of Miss Dearing in her room all those miles off down shadowy passageways—so I climbed back up & ventured a little way along the upstairs landing. At least the windows on the Grand Staircase let in a bit of light. I didn't let my eyes travel as far down as the Japanese Worrier but kept looking straight ahead.

That's when I saw her—walking away at the far end—tall & grey. Like an olden-days lady.

I wasn't looking out of the corners of my eyes.

I stared so hard my EYEBALLS ACHED—& then I blinked. She was gone. All except for a bit of her skirt disappearing round a door.

It was Miss Dearing—I am <u>convinced</u> of that. (I AM!)

Miss D. pacing round in the middle of the night. She's what woke me. Poor thing! Must be so worried—about the letters—or the donkeys getting out—or Mr Oak & his stubborn nature—or all of those things. I don't blame her.

LATER

I decided I would go back down the cellar ON MY OWN. If I could get up in the night to go looking for a noise I could do anything. Better than Shivering in your Shoes & doing nothing.

I took a lamp this time. My torch is getting v. weak (I need to get a new battery) & anyhow only shines a narrow beam. I pulled the tea-chest & all the other stuff aside & pushed it out the way. Whoever stored that there wasn't thinking of using the cellar.

Or maybe they were hoping to keep everyone else out!!

It was even spookier without Ella for company. This time I could see how old & worn the steps were & how much they curved round so you couldn't see what was ahead. The lamp gave out a jiggly sort of glow cos I couldn't keep my hand steady. It spun light & shadows over the cobwebby walls.

Just imagine Ella's face when I tell her! Nancy Parker being the logical scientifick one—taking it all one step at a time, noticing archways to right & left—a change in the floor here—a draft of fresh air there. I looked for more footprints but nothing was clear. The further I explored & no COLD HAND grabbed me by the shoulder & no COLD BREATH blew in my ear—the better I felt. The braver I felt.

What I found:—
- A big store for wine with a few v. dusty bottles left. I was right! (Thanks to Lady Pouncey!)
- Lots of the archways stuffed with old furniture & rusted tools & rolled up carpets. Looked like the mice & the beetles & even the toadstools have been having fun with them!!

- 3 windows bricked up almost all the way—but with a bit of light at the top
- Another door at the other end of the cellar. Bigger & wider than the one we found before. <u>Locked</u>. <u>No key fitted</u>.

I was getting cold & the archways full of creepy shadows were giving me the shivers again. I went back the way I came & then carried on to the other door. The footprint had vanished! Or been smudged into the rest of the floor. Which meant <u>somebody else</u> had been here.

I went thru my keys again tho I had to set the lamp down to do it. I put my hand on the door to steady myself & that's when it happened.

The door was NOT LOCKED.

It swung inwards all of its own accord!!

Dear Ella,

I think you will be v. supprised to hear I have been down
the Cellar again—alone! You may also be supprised that
when I tried the door again I found it OPENED!! There
was a small dark tunnel beyond. I did not explore any
further. I decided it would be too risky on my own & the
door could shut behind me—or someone could shut me in!
I have discovered another door at the opposite end—but
that one was locked. More when we next meet.

N.P.

Dear Nancy,

In the excitement of our investigations I forgot to
mention that Madame Arcana, a famous spiritualist
and medium, is in town next week to hold a public
audience. Children are not allowed in. However, I have
a sneaky idea about that. But you must go! We can
disguise you as a grieving wife or mother; you are
tall enough. Under a thick black veil no one will ever
know your age.

I am not absolutely sure what it is that mediums do,
but you may be able to speak to Madame Arcana. We
might find out if you are indeed sensitive to strange
phenomena. Of course, she may be an out-and-out
fraud and with your powers of detection you may be
able to tell that straight away. I realize I am not being
entirely rational here. Father would be very scathing if
he read this letter. But we must explore every avenue.

Meet me at the Public Library in Seabourne at half-
past two on Wednesday afternoon. I will bring the
disguise. Tell Miss Dearing you simply must have
the afternoon off but don't say why.
Yours, in fearful anticipation,

Ella Otter

40. FAIR PLAY

Ella glanced up at the owl in Miss Chard's office. 'Me again,' she murmured.

'What was that?' snapped Miss Chard.

Ella looked blank, with an added hint of extreme innocence. She noticed that Miss Chard was holding her second essay, the one that came to exactly two well-behaved pages.

'I'm pleased to say we have made some progress with your attitude, Eleanor. Let us hope this continues.'

'Yes, Miss Chard,' Ella chanted. She clasped her hands neatly behind her back. Her fingers were crossed.

'No more reports of difficulties from your teachers. Your form teacher, Miss Canning, is satisfied with the way you are settling in. Given this improvement I shall not, at this point, be taking up matters with your father.'

I wish you would, thought Ella, then he would see what a horror you are.

'But no resting on your laurels, Eleanor. You still have a long way to go to become a valued member of this school. There are other girls in the Third Form you should look to as an example—' She paused and frowned, as if struggling to come up with any, then hurried on—, 'Plenty of older girls, too. Girls who not only work hard and get good marks but are responsible, well-behaved, kind to others; who act as leading lights in our school world. Girls like Juniper Vale. Juniper gave an excellent speech at the Founder's Day hockey match. A copy is posted outside this room. You would do well to study it.'

Outside in the corridor Ella screwed up her fists, gritted her teeth, and glared very fiercely at a large framed photo of the school's Founder on the wall. One Word for the Day wasn't sufficient. She needed a whole string of them. She began with 'Woefully ignorant—utterly deluded—*rambunctiously bamboozled!*'

Beneath the photograph was the speech that Juniper Vale had written, headed 'Three Cheers for School!' It began,

'Fair play is at the very beating heart of our school . . .'

Ella groaned. When did Juniper Vale ever play fair? She read on. The speech was 'high old ham' as her father would say: full of cheap and easy phrases, regardless of the truth, praising school to the skies. No wonder Miss Chard liked it! Ella hated every word. Even the handwriting annoyed her, with its silly fussy tails to every *y* and *g*.

She was still standing there, fuming, when a prefect wandered round the corner and stopped short.

'Are you a Third Former? What are you doing out of lessons?'

Ella's jaw was too tight to speak.

'Have you just been to see Miss Chard?'

Ella nodded.

The older girl softened. 'Well, get off to where you should be right away. And do cheer up. The look on your face would turn someone to stone!'

41. SUSPICIOUS

NANCY'S JOURNAL

I was not entirely truthful in that letter I sent Ella. I couldn't step into that Tunnel—becos I was <u>Terrified</u>. Felt exceedingly brave when I went down there but then got the wind up so bad I didn't investigate properly.

But somebody might have left that door open deliberately. Somebody might be lying in wait for me. Didn't know if there was a human waiting with a COSH to bop me over the head—or the ICY HANDS of a ghost waiting to clasp me round the neck. Either way I'd be left for Dead & <u>no one would ever know.</u>

A proper Detective would never turn & run. A proper Detective's got NERVES OF STEEL. (Nancy Parker's got nerves of Jelly.)

But now my eyes keep turning to people's feet. The Laundryman came & I looked at his boots before I looked in his face! I need to know who made that FOOTPRINT.

<u>My Observations so far:—</u>
- <u>Peg Shanto</u>: man-sized rubber boots. Can't check her footprints. Raining so hard they wash away.
- <u>Miss Dearing</u>: owns a pair of gumboots. They are very LADYLIKE, much smaller than my feet.

- Mr Oakapple: hobnail boots with canvas gaiters to keep off the wet. All I can say of his footprints is if you could find 2 of them would be very wide apart, he is so bandy.

No sign of Ears or Spud today. Miss D. said she thought they had some of their own business to see to. I think it's the rain that's put them off.

Alfred Lubbock came round to see if Miss Dearing wanted another lesson in the Motor Car. I even looked at HIS feet.

I am suspishus of everyone!!

42. LINE OF INQUIRY

NANCY'S JOURNAL

At last I managed to catch Alfred's Ma when she had time to talk. I went to pay the bread bill & there she was sweeping up the yard between the Mill and the house. All the tables & chairs had been put away for the winter. She looked glad to stop for a while & chat.

She said 'This is where I serve the teas. It looks so pretty—tho you'd scarcely think it now. But then you wouldn't bileve how different Oxcoombe is come summer!'

Which was a perfect way for me to inquire about the village. I tried not to sound too mean—saying it was QUIET and RESERVED (not dead silent and unfriendly)—but then she piped up: 'Oh I'm a Seabourne girl myself—only came here when I married. You won't hurt my feelings if you speak plainly. I know how dull Oxcoombe can be!!'

She said in summer there's always trippers from Seabourne & people on bikes or hikers stopping by—even crowds in open-topped buses come to picnic & dip their toes in the sea. But when they all go home it's rather lonely. Specially now that Alfred works in his uncle's Garage & lives in rooms above. 'It's nice to have a cheery young face like yours around,' she said. (I felt v. bad for my face has not been particularly cheery of late!) Most folk in the village are old. Mrs Lubbock did not actually say OLD MISERIES—becos she is a nice woman. Nicer than me at any rate!

'There's one called Miss Violet Cummings who must be nearly 100! Used to work at the Grange as a seamstress in her youth.'

'How do the old folk feel about a new owner there?' I asked. That's when my Detective's nose twitched—for she did not say anything right away—and she sort of changed her face so I couldn't see what she really thoght. 'They will get used to it,' she said at last.

'And the donkeys?' That made her laugh. 'They may even get used to the donkeys,' she said.

'Even Miss Violet Cummings?' Again Mrs Lubbock put on that careful face. 'She's seen lots change in her lifetime.'

I tried to talk about the Shantos too, but all I got was 'You asked about them before'—as if she was sups suspishus. Then she changed the subject, saying what nobody cared for was the noise & smoke of that Mrs Vale's motor car tearing thru the village. (Turns out the Vales are quite new round here too. They live in Oriel House which is that white one halfway up the steep hill.) Mrs Vale is the one who nearly pitched Ella off her bike.

'Then they won't like Miss Dearing driving neither,' I put in. But it seems her car—Mr Duggan's motor—is such an old model it just putters along & everyone is used to it. 'What about her red & yellow cart?' I asked. 'Miss Dearing is Flam-boy-yant,' Mrs Lubbock replied. 'Brings a bit of colour to the place.' A LOT OF COLOUR I'd say.

I didn't get everything I wanted to know but I did get something. On the walk back I kept thinking about Miss Violet Cummings—100 years old—who used to work at Oxcoombe Grange.

- She must have VIEWS about Miss Dearing.
- And views about the neat gardens of the Grange being turned over to a Donkey Sanctury.
- Alfred's Ma was very careful with her words. In truth Miss Violet Cummings probbly hates change.
- She probbly hates donkeys.
- She's bound to have old-lady handwriting—cramped & hard to read.
- That makes her top suspect Nasty-Letter-Writer!

I was very pleased with this LINE OF INQUIRY & tried to work out how to pursue it further. Then I reached Oxcoombe Grange—where one of the donkeys was leaning over the wall—the smallest one that Peg calls Little Jem. Someone was standing in the lane & Little Jem was stretching his neck as far as it would go to reach the apples that person was feeding him.

'It's only windfalls,' she says—turning to me all gilty as if she should not be giving donkeys treats. 'He's such a dear tiny thing.' She was a tiny thing herself. Wrinkled like a windfall apple too. 'You work at the house—don't you?' she asked so I introduced myself all nice & polite.

She wiped the withered old hand she'd been feeding the donkey with & held it out for me to shake. 'I'm Miss Cummings. Violet Cummings.'

Which just goes to show that Detective Work is never straight-forward. I don't beleve I shall be pursuing that particular Line of Inquiry any further.

43. BACKSTAIRS RESEARCH

Ella was disappointed. This wasn't what she'd planned. She'd wanted a secret bird's-eye-view of Madame Arcana's performance, and she knew where she could get it. There was a window on the stairs at the back of the museum, looking into the big meeting hall. No one ever came there, no one would see her spying; it was the perfect place.

But when she got there she saw that it was very small. And very grimy. No one had cleaned it in years. Worst of all, it was much too high. Ella looked around. The stairs were a dumping ground for anything not wanted in the museum or the library. She tried standing on a box of old magazines, then on top of a display case of tattered butterflies, and then on the two balanced precariously together. All she could do was grab the windowsill with her fingertips, bringing down a shower of dust and filth.

'Damn, damn, damn,' she muttered, rubbing her eyes and spitting out dirt. She could hear what was going on inside the hall in a muffled sort of way but that was all. A spatter of applause, voices here and there, but nothing that she could properly make out.

She slumped on a box of books and waited. Her right foot went to sleep. She had a crick in her neck and cramp just about everywhere. Across from her was a case with a collapsed shelf inside it and a tumble of objects at the bottom. She stared idly at a label stuck on to the glass. It was yellowed and the print very faded. But finally she made out the words, 'Gift of Mr D. Duggan, Oxcoombe Grange.' She squinted at the contents: small carved figures, horses and humans and possibly a bear. The label didn't give any useful information about them. 'Of course it didn't,' Ella imagined her father remarking dryly. She rubbed at the dusty glass with her sleeve. The piled-up creatures looked rather familiar.

Suddenly the sound of a girl shouting came quite clearly from Madame Arcana's hall! Then doors banged, one after another, accompanied by a blast of angry voices. What on earth was going on? At least Nancy was inside to take note of everything. Unless it was Nancy who had stormed out—or been unmasked as a sceptic and *thrown* out!

And then the sound of a motor engine right outside drowned everything. Ella waited for it to pull away or stop. It didn't.

She scrabbled up the stairs. Her notebook fell to the ground and her pencil went rolling away into the darkness. There was a second window—this one long and thin—which she could see out of, just about, if she stretched up on tiptoe and got her elbows on the sill. She found herself looking down into the yard at the back of the building. There was a large car directly below her. Its bonnet was dark red. With a stutter, the engine noise died. As it did Ella felt as if she was suddenly encased in extra-quiet.

A woman stepped out of the car. From Ella's high window it was impossible to see her face, but the way she held her head, nose in the air, was unmistakable.

A door into the back of the building opened and Mrs Vale disappeared inside.

What was Juniper Vale's mother doing entering the hall where a famous medium was performing? Not at the front door where everyone else went, but at the back? Perhaps Ella's afternoon was not wasted after all.

44. MADAME ARCANA

NANCY'S JOURNAL

So at long last I have had a chance to try out my acting again—as a GREEVING RELATIVE at the Public Audience with Madame Arcana!

I must say Ella's got some nerve. Not only did she skip afternoon school by faking a swollen face & saying she had an appointment with the Dentist—she also smuggled out an old black coat of Mrs Prebble's & a thick veil for me to wear—all in her school bag! Then she talked the woman who runs the Libary into lending us the key to the staff cloakroom which is where I changed into my Greef-Stricken Lady disguise.

Mrs Prebble may be as tall as me—but she is much bigger round the middle—the coat was HUGE. It took some time to pin the veil on my hat too. I was somewhat red in the face by the time we finished & sweating inside my black gloves. (I 'borrowed' them from Miss Dearing's dressing-table drawer.)

Hat with dotty mourning veil (for added cover!)

Mrs Prebble's (big, long black) coat

Handkerchief for expected tears

Gloves

But Ella said 'Perfect! Your own mother wouldn't know you.' Then she bit her lip cos she knows I don't have a mother any more. Just like her. Ella was just a baby when she lost her mum—but I was old enough to remember mine.

There were lots of people in the hallway & by the time I paid for my ticket & went inside all the best seats were taken. It was the same place I'd come for that Lecture on Education but the crowd felt v. different. Sort of EXCITED & SCARED. I had to sit near the back—which turned out fine as I could see the ordience as well as the Stage & I spotted a number of Familiar Faces. I was a bit shocked at how many wanted a message from Madame Arcana. I noticed Mrs Shanto and Peg down near the front—mostly cos being tall Peg stuck up above the rest. She wasn't wearing a hat neither—just a scarf tied round her hair—all blue & pink & green. Made a change from all the poor souls in deepest black. (Like me.)

I wondered if they came hoping for some word from poor old Thumbs or Edward?

Then it went hushed & the stage curtains slid back—slow & creaking—as if someone was winding the handle with an achy arm. They came to a stop halfway. A gasp went up as a figure appeared between them: Madame Arcana herself.

I don't know what I expected a MEDIUM to look like— except not like this. She reminded me of Mrs Hooper down our street at home. Very plain & nothing out the ordinary. She even had that bump in her nose that Mrs Hooper's got. But Madame Arcana's dress made up for her face: a purple tent covered in black swirls with long sleeves like wings that fell right over her hands.

I expected someone to come on & make an announcement like at the Lecture. But Madame A. just started humming— then talking in a funny voice. After a while I thought: I know your game! I could tell she just said any old thing to see if it made sense to someone in the crowd. Like— 'Is there anyone here whose name begins with D?' Of course every Dinah and Dora in the place beleved it was going to be a message for them. Or—'I see a man in a white shirt and red tie.' Well, that is not an uncommon sight & somebody always put up their hand. The messages were very dull. 'He says to tell you he is in a happier place.' 'He looks down and sees you & wants you to be well & happy.' There was always a lot of 'happy'. A lot of sniffles & sighs in the hall too. Plus much use of hankerchiefs. I was right to carry one & make a good show of it.

I kept thinking how I'd report back to Ella—how I'd copy Madame Arcana's voice & make Ella laugh.

'I see two young men,' Madame Arcana was saying—chanting almost. 'Great fine fellows. Boys any family would be proud of.' All of a sudden a <u>great loud angwished cry</u> came from down the front. It was Mrs Shanto. She jumped up out of her seat & I could see her battered hat and nasty old coat with its ratty fur collar that gives you the shivers. (Whatever animal that fur is from it isn't in a HAPPY PLACE now!) (It's round Mrs Shanto's neck!!)

Madame Arcana waved her arm one way. 'I see the Battle of the Somme.' Then the other arm the other way. 'I see the mud of Ypres.' More howls from Mrs Shanto. 'I see brave boys cut down in their prime.'

Well—she'd chosen the <u>biggest deadliest battle-grounds</u> of the war. There was bound to be somebody here affected. Mrs Shanto was a-wailing and a-sobbing & I could tell the rest of the ordience was very wound-up.

'I see the letter W' Madame Arcana called out over their heads. Mrs Shanto stopped. She took her hands down from her face & said 'Not E? Not T?' The crowd went silent—hanging on the next words. Madame Arcana made her voice wobble even tho it stayed loud. 'The letter is so unclear—it's blurred—tear-stained—it's—'

But another voice shouted out 'Enough!' Peg Shanto was standing up now. She towered over her mother & she turned to the ordience. 'Enough lies,' she went on, quieter. 'Never should have come.' Then she took her mum by the shoulders (and the ratty fur) & helped her up the gangway & out the hall. I saw Peg's face as she went past. Her cheeks were even redder than usual & she put her head down like she didn't want anybody to see.

There was uproar in the crowd. Madame Arcana stood like a statue, but something about her expresshun told me she wasn't upset by it. Not upset at all. Thrilled more like.

Then she stuck out her arm again pointing to the back of the room. A few people turned but there was nothing to see. 'My strength is fading fast' she said. 'But one last vision. I see a child missing its mother. A sad child who cannot understand where she has gone. Don't worry, child! She is looking down on you. Your mother will always take care of you—no matter what <u>dark places</u> you stray into—

and what <u>dark forces</u> pull you towards them.'

Her purple arm with its sleeve that fell down over her hand lifted slowly—so many rings! —& she wiped her brow. She gave a big sigh. With a sad smile up at the ceiling she croaked out in a weary tone: 'Goodnight! Godspeed! Goodnight!'

I didn't know if she was talking to us or some Spirits we couldn't see.

With that she was gone. Everyone sat there staring at the gap in the curtains with their mouths hanging open.

Ella was nowhere to be found in the crowds afterwards. Just as well. I didn't feel like making her laugh with my impreshun of Madame Arcana. Not any more. Not after Peg had to take poor Mrs Shanto outside. And certainly not after that last message. She didn't <u>exackly</u> point at <u>me</u>. And I suppose there were plenty of people in that room who had lost their mothers. She didn't even say if she was talking about a boy or a girl—just a child. But it gave me the shivers all the same—& not like Mrs Shanto's fur collar does. And when she said 'dark places' that's when I shivered worst of all.

45. A SINGLE LIGHT

NANCY'S JOURNAL

It was almost dark by the time I got off the train at Oxcoombe & really dark as I made my way down the lanes towards the village & the Grange.

I wish I had never agreed to that plan of Ella Otter's. I wish I had the fore-site to bring Miss Dearing's torch. I am not used to living in the countryside yet. I am not used to living in A HAUNTED HOUSE. Cos it's all very well being Sientifick in broad day-light. But when it's dark & you're tired & a woman in a purple robe who thinks she's in touch with the Dead just pointed at you—a stranger—& told you things about yourself that are true . . . well then it's much harder to keep the SHIVERY FEELINGS at bay.

There was not a single light at the Grange when I got there. Miss Dearing had gone to give a talk & said she would not be back for tea.

As I walked up the path to the backyard I began to feel Un-Easy—as if I had Spiders crawling up & down my spine. I kept wanting to look back over my shoulder but I knew it was too dark to see anything if I did.

And then a little crack of light showed. Not from the Grange—from the room next to the Coach-house where they keep all the harnesses. A line of golden light that made me feel weak with releef. I didn't have to go into that dark old house all on my own. I took no care about how much noise I made as I approached—the more noise the better in fact! But something made me stop in my tracks before I got there. I had one hand reached out for the door & that hand FROZE.

Cos what I heard from inside the Harness Room was CRYING. The real sort of tear-up-your throat hard crying you do when you think no one can hear you. When you know there's nobody around to hear. When you're perfectly ALONE.

I was stuck. I actually teetered on my feet as if I was about to fall inside, shoving that door open & causing a terrific shock to whoever was there. But I didn't wobble & I didn't shove that door open. I calmed myself down. Even those spiders stopped running up & down my spine.

It was Peg Shanto inside crying her heart out—about what Madame Arcana said, about her mum, about those poor brothers of hers dead on the fields of France.

I couldn't say anything to her. I couldn't say I was there too & I knew what her tears were about. Cos the Nancy that attended that show of the medium's—she was dressed up as another Greeving Widow or Sister or Mum. Which isn't true.

I crept away across the yard, fumbled at the back

door & let myself in to that dark kitchen without more ado. There was a glow of last embers coming from the Excelsior. I could have sat down & cried myself—but there was work to do. Keeping yourself busy drives all sorts of horrors away.

46. DESPERATE TYPES

Ella crouched in the shadows between two huge metal dustbins. The smell was vile. She had a new sort of cramp in her legs now and a different crick in her neck. But she had to stay where she was for as long as it took. There was no point in giving up now. She was on the trail of something, even if she didn't know what it was. Mrs Vale and Madame Arcana . . . a most unexpected pairing . . . they must be up to something. In fact, Ella *wanted* them to be up to something because she longed to catch the Vales out in wrongdoing. It was about time Juniper or her mother got their comeuppance. 'Follow your instincts, Ella Otter,' she muttered to herself, and blew on her fingers to stop them going numb. She had lost her gloves *again*.

Mrs Prebble isn't going to forgive me this time, she thought, and an image of the kitchen at home, warm and cosy, the lamps lit, the table set for tea, came instantly to mind. There might be an apple cake baking, and there would certainly be raspberry jam . . .

She must have leaned too heavily against one of the bins and tipped it, for a lid came crashing down. It rolled into the middle of the yard like a cartwheel and fell down flat with a terrible jangling sound. Just then the door she had been watching opened.

The woman who stepped out paused. She looked shocked—and suspicious.

'Just cats,' said Mrs Vale, who followed on her heels. 'Or seagulls.'

In contrast to Mrs Vale's abundant furs and fussy hat the other woman was dressed very plainly in a long dark coat and a headscarf. Her face, or as much as Ella could see of it in the failing light, was very plain too. No distinguishing features. If I had to identify her again I doubt I could do it, she thought.

'I'm quite worn out,' the other woman said. She slumped against the side of the motor car while Mrs Vale opened the passenger door for her.

'Of course you are, Maud. But you said it went well.'

'Very well. Very well indeed. I shall have lots of enquiries for personal audiences after this. So many desperate fools.'

She climbed up into the car. Ella saw a flash of purple at the end of her coat-sleeve, a ruffle of purple silk about her ankles. Then she was inside and the door shut.

'What on earth—?' Mrs Vale had spotted the dustbin lid in her way. She picked it up in her gloved hand and carried it fastidiously towards the bins. Ella shrank back, clutching her satchel to her chest in case the bright yellow badge on her blazer showed up. What on earth would Mrs Vale make of a Grammar School girl hidden behind the Assembly Rooms' bins?

But Mrs Vale wasn't looking; she let the lid drop into place and turned on her heel. 'Desperate fools,' she murmured, and let out a low chuckle.

As soon as the car had pulled away Ella climbed out of her hiding place. Her gloves were gone and her school uniform stank of unspeakable things. She had missed countless trains home and Mrs Prebble would undoubtedly have words to say. But it had all been worth it.

The Seabourne Herald
YESTERDAY'S EVENTS

A SALE OF WORK was held by the Sussex Ladies' Action Committee to raise funds for a number of local good causes. The sum of £17. 7s. 6d was raised.

After tea Miss E. M. Dearing gave a talk on animal welfare vivaciously entitled, 'Must we carry on taking donkeys for a ride?'

A PUBLIC AUDIENCE before a packed crowd was held by the medium, Madame Arcana, in the Seabourne Assembly Rooms. Well-known in London circles, it is understood Madame Arcana will also be giving private audiences at The Grand Hotel.

Following the event, one lady, who wished to remain anonymous, said, 'The messages were very touching. My dear mother has received great comfort.' Another commented, 'All stuff and nonsense!'

Madame Arcana will be appearing in Brighton next week.

7. A SORT-OF PLAN

'Pay attention, Eleanor!' Miss Canning said sharply.

This was the third or fourth time Ella had heard that phrase today. Possibly the fifth. The only thing she was counting were the minutes until school ended. She had a plan. A sort-of plan. She was going to call on the Vales. It might not be a formal visit. It might be more like a break-in. She really wouldn't know until she got there.

At home, she was about to dash up the stairs and change out of her school uniform (which, despite Mrs Prebble's efforts, still had a vaguely *off* smell about it) when she spotted the collecting tin on the hall table. It had a rather bad picture of a donkey pasted round it and contained— to Ella's sure knowledge—two pennies and a sixpence.

She decided to stay in her uniform. Her satchel lay just inside the front door where she had dropped it. Going on blind instinct, she emptied everything out on the floor—textbooks, exercise books, pens, pencils, ruler, ink-stained handkerchief, liquorice pinwheels and sherbet lemons—then threw back in a notebook, pencil, and a handful of sweets for sustenance. She had no idea how long her plan would take to carry out.

'Just off out again,' she called, scrunching her school hat on her head. 'Shan't be long.'

Mrs Prebble came out of the kitchen and gave her a stern look. 'Don't be. Last night was bad enough.'

Ella shook the tin. 'I promised Miss Dearing,' she said, and ran.

She made sure that Mrs Prebble didn't see her taking her bike from round the side of the house.

The gates to Oriel House stood wide open. Ella slid off her bicycle and pushed it into the hedge until it was well and truly hidden. Over the hedge, further down the hill, she could see a girl riding a brown pony. The way she held her head looked like Juniper; the way she set the pony again and again at a high jump and used her stick on its rump looked very much like Juniper. So at least she knew that Juniper was out of the way.

Ella took a deep breath and turned towards the house. Its dark windows stared back inscrutably. The drive was empty of cars. Perhaps no one else was at home? Mrs Vale was bound to have servants, but they could be snoozing or reading the afternoon paper with their feet up. She might be able to sneak in unnoticed.

Clutching her collecting tin to the front of her school blazer, Ella marched up to the front door. But she didn't immediately ring the bell. There was a long narrow panel beside the door, glass panes of different colours. She peered through a yellow one, which seemed the most transparent. A black-and-white shape was moving inside. Ella peered through the next pane, pale-green. The shape was a housemaid, who stopped what she was doing and stared, then came towards the door. Ella straightened up, and tried to look keen and eager.

'I'm collecting for good causes,' she announced, with a toothy smile. The maid just gave her back a grumpy stare.

'I'm a friend of Juniper's. We go to the same school.' For the first time ever Ella was glad to be in the unmistakable maroon-and-mustard with touches of sky-blue of the Girls' Grammar.

The maid had a grumpy voice to match her face. 'Miss Juniper's out riding. She won't come in 'til it gets dark.'

'Is Mrs Vale there? Or anyone else I can speak to?' She jingled the tin optimistically, keeping her hand over the picture of the donkey. She didn't think many people were as fond of them as Miss Dearing was.

The maid scrutinized Ella and her uniform again, then stepped back to let her in, saying, 'If you'd care to follow me.'

At least I am *in*, Ella thought. Which was where her plan sort of ran out . . .

48. ADMIRING THE VIEW

The room she was asked to wait in had a large window with a view of Oxcoombe village, stretching from the beach to the watermill, with Oxcoombe Grange right in the middle. She could easily make out the donkey pens and chicken houses, even the white blobs of geese asleep on one of the terraces. What was in that letter Nancy had showed her? 'Disgraceful . . . like a gypsy encampment'?

Ella turned from the view and surveyed the rest of the room, trying to think like a detective. She might only have minutes before the maid came back or Mrs Vale appeared. There was a bookcase and an armchair and an unlit fire, a painting of horses over the mantelpiece. There was a writing desk with the usual arrangement of leather-edged blotter and inkwell and letter-rack. All very ordinary.

But—*blotter*, Ella thought. You could pick up clues from the marks left by ink on blotting paper. The writing was reversed, of course, and only showed if the ink was truly wet when blotted. She peeled the top sheet of blotting paper out and turned it this way and that, trying to make sense of the marks. They looked like nothing more than bird footprints in snow. Except . . .

Were those marks an *O* and a *G*? *Ox*... and *Gr*...*g*? Oxcoombe Grange! It couldn't be anything else. Why was Mrs Vale writing about Oxcoombe Grange? The answer was obvious. Ella looked up from the writing desk at the wonderful vista: sea, sky, and herds of donkeys. Oriel House was designed to make the most of the views, and now almost every window was forced to look at this! Mrs Vale must be furious, and she wasn't the sort ever to give way. She must be writing anonymous letters to try to shame Miss Dearing into changing things. Or, better still, to drive her out!

Ella rolled the vital sheet into a tube and fastened it safely inside her satchel. A grumpy cough behind her made her whirl round. The maid said, 'Mrs Vale will be free to see you in a few minutes, if you don't mind waiting, miss.' Ella squeezed out a grateful smile and was left alone again. She glanced down at her collecting tin with the sad-looking donkey on the label. There was no chance that Mrs Vale would contribute to that cause; she'd probably throw Ella out of the house. Besides, Ella had found out enough to be going on with. It was better to creep away now . . .

Taking great care, she opened the door to the hall just a crack. The maid was still there, dusting a table full of ornaments, cleaning and replacing every piece methodically. It would take her ages.

Ella shut the door and scanned the room again. To

one side of the bookcase was another door. She was trying the handle when she heard muffled voices beyond. The handle turned smoothly and the door slid open an inch, without a squeak: the housemaid was obviously very thorough in her work.

A woman's voice was saying, 'All nonsense, of course.' A different voice replied, with a sharp little laugh, 'True, it's just a bit of fun to pass the time. But you never know. Perhaps I *do* have psychic powers.'

Ella put her eye to the gap. All she could see was a pair of hands dealing out cards on a table. She couldn't see the woman who owned them, but there were heavy rings on the fingers and purple ruffles at the wrist. One card was turned up, placed in a semicircle like a game of Patience, then another.

The first voice said, 'For heaven's sake, don't tell me what it's supposed to mean. There's a visitor I must see, and then I'll drive you into town.'

'Wait!' said the second voice. One be-ringed hand paused, hovering over the tabletop. 'Look at that: a secret—a child—an old enemy. There's a warning in the cards.'

'A warning—really, Maud! Do you think I'm one of those gullible women you prey on.'

The hands instantly gathered up the cards and shuffled them together. 'That *I* prey on? Vera, *you* are the one who knows Seabourne. *You're* the one who has found all those willing fools for me.'

'That's as may be, sister. But *you're* the one who needs the cash those willing fools are so eager to hand over. It's really only pocket money for me. Dear Percival looks after me very nicely. Which is why I can drive you about in my marvellous new motor car. Now, be ready to leave in five minutes.'

Ella heard firm heels across a wooden floor and a door opening and shutting. She flew away from *her* door and struck a rapt pose at the window, as if admiring the view. There was no sign of Juniper and her pony. Purple clouds were collecting over the sea; a few raindrops dashed against the glass like arrows.

Mrs Vale swept in. 'Juniper's little friend, I understand? What is it you're collecting for?'

Ella held out the tin, donkey foremost. She was right. Mrs Vale wasted no time in showing her the door.

She stepped outside just as the first crackle of lightning cut the sky. A great gust of wind whipped the *porridge pot* off her head and swept it high over the cliffs and out to sea. She felt needles of rain pummelling into her bare scalp—and smiled.

49. MISS DEARING GOES MOTORING

NANCY'S JOURNAL

Ella Otter & her bike showed up at the kitchen door in the middle of a Thunderstorm—dripping water all over the floor—babbling about cards & warnings & blotting paper. She was really quite raving—rolling her eyes at me & hissing 'The letters! I know who wrote them. I've got evidence!'

Before I could hear any more Miss Dearing sent me to fetch a towel—dashed back so I didn't miss anything. I was on pins. Had Ella forgotten that she wasn't supposed to know anything about the ANONYMOUSE LETTERS? That Miss Dearing didn't even know I knew!? I flung the towel at Ella in a most un-grashus way & pulled the biggest warning face I could.

Ella got a tin out of her school satchel & banged it on the table. (Not much in it from what I heard & the label was all blurry with wet.) 'I was out collecting for the donkeys. I called on Mrs Vale—you know—up the hill.'

'Oh the Vales,' Miss Dearing said & not in her usual kindly tone.

'She had a lady with her & I over-heard what they

were saying.' (Well I know what Ella means by OVER-HEARD—her ear would be pressed up against some door!) She went on to tell us that Mrs Vale's visitor was the medium, Madame Arcana. They're sisters & from what they said Madame Arcana's a right old fake & Mrs Vale is in leeg with her to trick people out of their money.

'Are you really surprised?' Miss Dearing asked. 'Do any of these dreadful people have Mystical Powers? Of course not. Ella—with your education—you should know better.'

'But—' Ella spluttered but couldn't say any more for Miss D. put the towel over her head & began drying her hair very ruffly.

Next she barked out an actual ORDER: 'Nancy—fetch the Cherry Linctus from my bedside table. Ella is going to need it—bound to catch a cold after a soaking like that. Not even wearing a hat!'

I had no chance to talk to Ella alone—when I got back Miss D. was getting ready to drive her home in the motor car! 'It's no night for riding a bycycle & her father must be wundering where she is.' It struck me that it was NO NIGHT for Miss Dearing to be motoring neither!

I followed them out to the yard. Ella (still in that towel) was turning the crank to start the motor while Miss Dearing clutched the steering wheel with her eyes popping out of her head. I looked out over Oxcoombe—just 2 or 3 dim lights wavering thru the pouring rain. If Miss Dearing was going to drive off into the night she wasn't leaving me on my own—and if we ended up in a ditch that was better than waiting here all night for her return!! (I did not care to think: what if we ended up DEAD in a ditch?!)

I managed to jump in the back seat before Miss Dearing pulled away—only to find I was sharing it with Ella's bike. I twisted myself up like a broken umbrella & just skweezed in round it. Miss Dearing bumped us down the drive to the road (fast & slow & stop & fast again) and Ella had to point out there was a lever to wipe the rain off the windscreen.

Thank goodness Miss Dearing chose not to take us up the steep hill—we drove along a long winding back road instead. I cannot say our journey was Without Incident. But we were not killed—otherwise I would not be writing this. (However I may have a few BRUSES from the bike.) The wind was tearing branches off the trees & throwing them about & there was water right across the lane in places. 'What an adventure!' Miss Dearing cried as at last we swerved round The Green.

The moment we stopped outside Ella's house Mrs Prebble ran out in the rain. She always comes across as v. calm but I could see that she had been at her Wit's End. She kept saying 'yet again!' & 'where on earth?' & suchlike.

THE 'SIGNS':

furrowed brows

untucked hair

agditated manner

crumpled apron

In contrast the Professor wandered out to ask 'What is going on? I can hardly hear myself think!'

Ella's tea was waiting for her under a cloth but—whatever it was—it stayed there & Mrs Prebble insisted on feeding us all hot soup, then hot Apple Cake (delishus) & cocoa. The Professor offered Miss Dearing a nip of brandy—she agreed!—& took one himself. Maybe he was MORE TROUBLED than he showed.

The Brandy made Miss Dearing even more cheerful—swearing that there was not much to driving a motor car & that she was now quite The Expert. She added 'But I think I have done enough for now. Nancy & I shall spend the night at Apple Cottage. The beds will need airing & the larder is bare—but hey ho. What fun!' (Phew!)

50. EGGS & BACON

NANCY'S JOURNAL

Up early this morning with rumbling insides & back to Oxcoombe—tho not before I had been across to ask after Ella. Mrs Prebble was just making up a breakfast tray for her & said she was not exactly ill but was having a day off school anyhow & was NOT TO BE DISTURBED. We could not talk last night under the ~~angs~~ ankshus eyes of Mrs Prebble & Ella's dad. So <u>still</u> not got to the bottom of what she was raving on about.

Miss Dearing drove down the steep hill to Oxcoombe with The Brakes <u>firmly applied</u>—even Pancho would have gone faster. The sun was up. Shining puddles lay everywhere & the sea sparkled.

'What a view! What a view!' Miss D. cried. I don't know if she meant Oxcoombe Bay or the gardens of the Grange filled with donkeys.

I did not want to spoil her good mood but felt I must speak out about Madame Arcana. She is taking money off people who can't afford it—& making fools of them that can! It's <u>not right</u> & I know Miss Dearing is very strong on RIGHT & WRONG.

When she saw the damidge the storm had done at the Grange her mood was spoiled anyway. But not for long. Next thing it was: 'Eggs on toast—Nancy—eggs on toast! We've much work to do & no one can work on an empty stummuck.' (I do wish Miss Dearing ate bacon! It was exackly the sort of morning that called for EGGS & BACON!!)

I poured her tea strong & then raised the subjeck of Mrs Vale & Madame Arcana again. 'Can't you do something, Miss? Say something? They trick poor greeving folk out of their hard-earned cash. Folk like Mrs Shanto. And Peg.'

That made her sit up. She wanted to know how I knew & I couldn't think of anything to say but I was there too. 'You Nancy? Why? Your Father came home from the war.'

I didn't say anything. I may have looked bit SHEEPISH. Could hardly say I was <u>investigating</u>. Then Miss Dearing put her hand over mine & looked sad. 'Oh I'm so sorry—I forgot you lost your mother.' I sort of wish she didn't know.

But at least the look on her face said she was thinking about it all. <u>Thinking hard.</u>

51. MY DISCOVERY

NANCY'S JOURNAL

I sat down & made a note of all that before my next task which was to go round the house & check for leaks & broken glass. I could see Mr Oakapple outside picking up twigs & branches. He appeared quite Forlorn. Miss Dearing was huddled with Peg talking about the animals. The fences look fine but one of the donkey shelters the Shanto boys put up is <u>flat on the ground</u> & the other seems pretty shaky. (The Hen Palace looks all right tho.)

At mid-morning I went to find Mr Oak & cheer him up with cake.

THAT IS WHEN I MADE MY DISCOVERY.

There's a terrace next to the house & below it is a bed of ivy with old statues poking out—ladies with their arms come off & gents with legs like goats. I always thought it was one of the creepiest bits of the garden. Great fronds of ivy grow down from the terrace above & up from the ground below. I suppose it's meant to look like a theatre with actors & curtains & all. But it's been disturbed by the Storm. One gentleman tipped over & huge bits of ivy snapped off & lying about. Where they left the wall clear I could see a pattern of archways in the brickwork—I could even see filthy-dirty glass at the top. I knew what it meant & it made my heart jolt!

These were the bricked-up arches in the cellar with tiny windows to let in a chink of light. I stood there dumfounded: I was staring at the outside of the cellar of Oxcoombe Grange!! You would never know—it was so WELL DIS-GIZED.

I gazed about to see if I could see where that tunnel ran as well—but the land fell away here in layers of garden. The only high bit was under the yard & the coach-house—and then it dipped—& it didn't come up again till the little hill the church was on.

Mr Oakapple came over & I was so excited I nearly told him what I'd found. Then I looked at his boots. You just never know.

In an Investigation You Must Keep your Suspishuns to Yourself

So instead I said 'Oh Mr Oakapple! Miss Dearing took me to a most fassinating lecture the other week about lady gardeners. It really made me think.' It was probbly a mistake to mention LADY GARDENERS. Mr Oak grunted & stumped off. Didn't even take his tea.

52. ESCAPED

Ella enjoyed breakfast in bed *and* the prospect of no school while others were toiling away at lessons. She enjoyed it when her father looked in to say goodbye and ask if she wanted anything; he was off to London, for a talk at the Royal Society. She enjoyed Mrs Prebble's concerned glances and her promise to nip into the middle of Seabourne for a new school hat to replace the one that had disappeared last night.

What she enjoyed most was the quiet in the house when they had both gone, with only the gentle click of Sausage's claws as he padded about searching for his master. She sprang out of bed and flung on her oldest clothes, stuffed some essential items into a rucksack, then ran downstairs where she scribbled a note for Mrs Prebble. Sausage watched her with great sad eyes.

'Sorry. You can't come with me this time,' Ella told him.

'I've got a plan!' Ella said, arriving at Nancy's kitchen door just as suddenly as last night, though this time dry and dressed for action. *Another* plan, she added, to herself. 'Come on. We've got masses to do.'

Nancy waved her dustpan and brush. 'You might've got masses to do but so have I. I work here, remember?'

'Everyone's busy outside. They'll never notice what you're up to.'

'They will when the dishes are dirty and the oven goes out.'

Ella shook her head impatiently. 'We are going down that tunnel!' she said, pulling a very businesslike torch out of her rucksack. 'I'm going to find out where it leads if it kills me.'

Nancy gave her a rather queasy glance in reply.

But Ella's persuasion worked. Nancy took off her apron and followed her into the passageway, saying, 'I've been thinking . . . have you still got the map you showed me?'

'Had to sneak it back into the reference library. I should never have taken it in the first place. Why?'

'Well . . . I drew a sort of copy—just from memory—but I may have I left something off it. D'you remember any faint, dotty lines?'

Ella didn't remember, and was too busy thinking about her next move. She heaved the tea-chest aside and switched on her torch. She could see that it wasn't really a cupboard, merely used as one. The steps to the cellar ran down from the right-hand side. Straight ahead would be the wall of the kitchen, and above, the servants' stairs. A small hook hung on the wall in front of her, a hook just perfect for keys. Empty.

'Coming?' she asked, and without waiting for an

answer set off down the steps.

The cellar was cold and somehow more drafty than before. Ella crept forward, swinging the torch-beam. Nancy was close behind her, whispering, 'I found out loads of stuff I haven't had time to tell you. Just this morning I—'

There was a loud crack. Ella felt Nancy's fingers grip her shoulder.

'What was that?'

The noise came again; then again, louder and faster. Nancy's grip gave way. 'Hammering. Outside. Spud Shanto must've arrived to fix the donkey shelter.'

'It sounds so close.'

'It is,' said Nancy. 'Look, see those archways with the bits of light at the top. I found out where they go. It's lighter now than last time I was down here. Usually there's ivy that grows down the outside, but the storm shifted it.'

Ella swung round and shone the light up on to their two faces. 'But—we're *underground*.'

Nancy shook her head. 'Most of this must be underground, but Mr Oakapple told me they dug things up and moved a load of earth and old stones when they made the garden. No expense spared. It was the fashion to have terraces and suchlike and Mr Duggan's grandad was mad to have the latest notions from abroad, and better'n anyone else.' She took a step backward. 'We ought to be under the old house here—' then several steps forward, almost out of the torchlight, 'and under the terrace here. But I don't understand why it's got archways.'

Ella was still trying to puzzle the layout of the house above them, when something struck her. 'The Priory!' What was it Professor Goring had said? *Some were destroyed outright and others were allowed to fall into ruin. Their stones were scavenged for building materials.* 'King Henry gave it to his friend for his private home. William de Warne must have built on top of the ruins of the old Priory!'

But Nancy was no longer listening.

'Over here,' she called. 'The door's still open.'

53. WHERE IT LEADS

Ella found herself clutching the torch so hard her fingers ached. As it was her idea, she was in the lead. Which was a good idea . . . wasn't it? She could hear Nancy breathing close behind her. Other than that the tunnel was as silent as the grave. It smelled of cold, clammy earth and stone; that was very grave-like, too. She played the torch-beam above her, then down at her feet.

'Narrow. Not much higher than our heads.'

'*Your* head,' Nancy replied, ducking.

'It slopes away here.'

Nancy bundled right into her back. They almost fell. 'See what you mean.'

The tunnel wove on, more or less straight, leading gradually downwards. To Ella it felt as if it was getting more cramped, more crushing, all the time. She shivered. The tunnel took a sudden turning to the right. They stopped, staring as the torch picked out the way ahead, dark, damp and dripping.

'D'you think we should go on?' she asked.

'Don't you want to know where it leads?'

'Ye-es.' Still Ella hesitated. 'That old chair you fixed

in the way, to stop the door shutting behind us—are you sure it's strong enough?'

'If you like I'll nip back and make sure,' suggested Nancy. 'Stuff some more bits of wood in there too.'

'Not without me. I've got the only torch.'

'We'll both go.'

They did.

'That's torn it,' said Nancy.

Ella shone the torch over the doorway—or, to be precise, the door. It was shut, with just a broken chair-leg lying where a whole chair had been, propping the heavy door open.

'Certainly has,' Ella agreed, trying to keep her voice steady.

On the back of the door was a small iron channel where a ring may once have hung. But there was no ring there now. She tried to pull at it, but her fingers could get no purchase. Nancy picked up the chair-leg and tried to lever it with that, but it was too big to fit. Rotten, too, for half of it fell off on to the floor.

Ella felt sudden prickles of sweat under her thick clothes. 'We're stuck,' she said. 'We could shout, I suppose, and bang on the door. They're all busy up there. How long would it take before anyone heard us?'

Nancy looked dubious. 'No one did anything when I said I heard noises.'

'Oh. Yes.' Ella stared down at her shoes, where the torch-beam hung disconsolately. 'I wish I'd brought Sausage after all. He would have barked his head off.'

Neither spoke for a minute. The dense silence of the tunnel settled around them. We might never get out of here, thought Ella.

'Madame Arcana gave me a message,' Nancy said suddenly. 'I never got to tell you that, neither. She said I would stray into *dark places*, and *dark forces* would pull me in.'

Ella swallowed hard. They both heard it. 'You know that Madame Arcana is an out-and-out, self-confessed, money-grubbing fraud!' she protested. But her voice wobbled.

'Then she told me my mum would always look after me,' Nancy said, and turned away, even though it was pitch-dark in that direction. 'So—if we can't go back, we must go on.'

They reached the right turn again, and walked carefully onwards.

'It's beginning to slope *up*!' Ella said after a while.

'It's not so cold, is it? Or is that just wishful thinking?'

A while longer and then Ella said, 'There's steps!'

She stopped, shining the torch upwards. The tunnel had come to an end. Stone steps twisted tightly away into the dark. Ella knew they had to climb them but she didn't move a muscle.

Beside her Nancy whispered, 'That old map. Don't know if I was imagining it. Maybe it was just smudges and stains, not part of the map at all . . .' She hesitated.

'Go on.'

'Well, it was after you pointed out the caves. And said it was all about smuggling. I was wondering if they were sort of other lines showing where they thought the smugglers went?'

'Who d'you mean by *they*?'

'Whoever made the map.'

Ella frowned. Who *had* made the map? 'I studied it jolly well. I think I'd remember lines. There was a mark like a boat.'

'Oh, that was the ferry,' Nancy said confidently. 'Before the bridge was built there was a ferry—and the Shantos used to run it.'

'You never told me this!'

'Never got a chance!'

Ella began to climb the steps now, cautiously. 'There's a trapdoor above me. I can see a bolt. But I can't reach it.'

'Lucky for us I'm taller,' said Nancy, reaching the top step beside her and stretching up. The bolt was well-oiled. It slid back with ease.

Ella and Nancy exchanged glances.

'We can get *out*,' Ella breathed. 'But where to? What if we fetch up in the middle of one of those cottages? Or in a cave—and the tide's in?'

Nancy was pushing at the trapdoor with the flat of both hands. 'Reckon—ugh —I can—ugh—probably pull you up after me.'

The trapdoor lifted and fell back with a crash. Both girls froze. The air seemed to vibrate with the noise.

There was a square of dim light above them. Then nothing—no movement, no sound. Except for two girls letting out their breath.

In silence Nancy levered herself out.

'Well?' Ella whispered, gazing up.

Nancy's head appeared at the trapdoor. 'Those lines on the map I saw—just little faint dots—I was right.' She stuck out a hand for Ella to grasp. 'They led to the church.'

54. THE EVIDENCE

NANCY'S JOURNAL

I am writing this at the kitchen table. Just taken Miss Dearing's supper on a tray into the Snuggery. Ella is hiding upstairs in my room. She plans to <u>stay the night.</u> She says it will be fine cos she left a note for Mrs Pebble & besides her Dad is away in London with load of other ~~Perfessors~~ Professors at a <u>Royal Society Dinner.</u> According to Ella they talk all night about the latest sientifick discoveries.

Our own Discoveries have been coming thick & fast. It was bad getting stuck in that Tunnel—but then we had to walk back from the church looking like nothing was up! It's quite common for Ella to go about all mud-stained—I am supposed to be the respecktable Housekeeper of Oxcoombe Grange.

But now we know OLDEN-DAY SMUGGLERS used that tunnel & someone must be using it again! <u>Often.</u> The oiled bolt proves that. I put this to Ella as we hurried back—trying to keep my voice as low as could be—you never know who might be earwigging from a window or behind a garden wall. Also trying not to be spotted by anyone til we got back inside the Grange. Specially as Ella was hiding a big torch under her jumper. But Peg saw us & gave me such an odd look!

We cleaned up in the Scullery (Ella scarcely looking any better when she finished. She would never make a <u>neat & tidy</u> maidservant— but then she'll never have to.) Then we snuck up the back stairs & she emptied her rucksack on my bed. Bits of pie & paper & pencils all fell out. Toffees & torch batteries. Rope & matches. Heaven knows what she

Ella Otter, Investigator

had planned. She held up a compass—'Should have taken this with us down the tunnel.' She still doesn't beleeve that I saw Smugglers' lines on that map.

But next out came THE EVIDENCE—a roll of paper covered in ink blots. From that wicked Mrs Vale's own writing table! I had the Anonymouse Letter tucked into this journal. There was an <u>Ox</u> and a <u>Gr</u> just like on the blotter. I passed it to Ella—she read it—then gave a yelp just like Sausage if you stood on his foot! She pointed to the pot-hooks on the *g* & the *y* of gypsy. Then all the other gs and ys. 'I've seen fussy tails like these somewhere before.' Her face went dark & her eyes squeezed up & she hissed a name: Juniper Vale.

Turns out Juniper Vale (who for some reason is v. well-regarded in Ella's school) wrote a speech that was pinned up for everyone to read. It was written in a most distincktive hand. And no matter how she's tried to diz-gize it in the Anonymouse Letter—those tails give her away!

Ella was spitting with rage. 'Nasty spiteful creature! Mrs Vale may not know about the letters but I bet these are just the words she uses. Juniper's been doing her dirty work for her. What a family! We should tell Miss Dearing—tho not yet. First we have to carry out my latest experiment & it's got to be tonight.'

I felt my heart sink.

'You do know what day it is—don't you?' she went on (giving me no time to reply) 'The last day of October. ALL HALLOW'S EVE! When they say there's scarcely a veil between this world and the next. If there's anything INHUMAN haunting the Grange you are bound to see it!!'

Don't like the sound of that. Not at all. Quite frankly the Last Thing I want to test out is whether I am really the sort who sees ghosts. And the other Last Thing I want to find out is that Oxcoombe Grange really is haunted. I didn't say this to Ella (speaking it OUT LOUD just makes it more scary!).

What I did say was there's deffinitely HUMANS up to no good—& scaring the daylights out of me—& we may well discover them too. Got my own Theory about that to do with bells & doors & thumps under the kitchen floor. Which is why I want to be on lookout duty near the door to the Cellar.

So we've put my Theory & Ella's idea together. We are going to lie in wait at Strat-ee-jick Places in the house. (That's what she called them.)

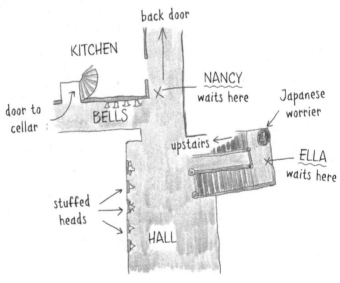

Soon as Miss Dearing's gone to bed we are to take up our posts. I shall have to wear that vest & Gran's lambs-wool girdle to keep out the shivers & stop my teeth from chattering!

55. LYING IN WAIT

Ella had a brilliant idea. It came as she crept up the stairs to the halfway landing, shielding her torch-beam with one hand. The sky beyond the window showed a sprinkle of stars. From here she ought to have a good view up *and* down, if anything moved about. She very much doubted that a ghostly presence would appear, but a solidly human one just might, so she couldn't afford to be seen. The only place to hide was behind the Japanese suit of armour. Unless, of course . . .

It took a while, and some effort, and a bit of clanking and creaking to wriggle into place. The torch had to be left at her feet. She found she wasn't tall enough to reach the visor so she had to squint out through the moustache. Time slid slowly by. It was very different to the daytime. Ella's ears were alert to tiny noises—the tick of a window pane as the breeze touched the glass, the faint click of old boards shifting on the upper landing, the thump of her own heart. The *upper landing*: that was where Nancy thought she saw ghosts in the shadows. Then it turned out that Miss Dearing in her old-fashioned night attire could be mistaken, in poor light, for someone from the past. Another logical explanation.

Soon she was feeling cramped and uncomfortable, even more so than crouched on boxes at the museum, trying to spy on Madame Arcana's performance. She remembered the cases of tattered butterflies and that heap of small figures, the 'gift of Mr Duggan'. Two pictures collided in her brain: the gift of Mr Duggan and the little clay horse that Professor Goring was so fond of. There was a connection—if she could only remember . . .

A muffled thump put it out of her mind. Where did the noise come from? Up? Down? It was hard to hear very well from her hiding place. She peered out, waiting for a sign from Nancy's torch.

Nothing.

Was it the sort of thump a person would make? Or a being from beyond the veil, the veil that was at its *thinnest* on this very night?

Another thump. A faint cry.

Ella's blood froze. The hairs stood up on her neck. Nancy was right to be worried about living in this house! Was that cry from Nancy? Or was it from the ghost?

Something was moving in the hall below. A terrible soft dragging noise, like a body that could barely pull itself along. Or be pulled along . . . Nancy hadn't signalled to her. Was the body *Nancy's*?

Ella glanced upwards—she might be able to make her escape that way—and saw something in the gloom, floating over the stairs. A ghastly apparition! Not grey, but cobwebby white, with long white draggled hair.

She tried to move but her arms were trapped, her legs as heavy as lead. Yet she *had* to run. She made one last supreme effort, heaving herself forward. Thump! Bump! Thump! Noise crashed all about her. Stars plucked out of the night sky began spinning round her head.

A cry broke out, followed by another, and the pounding of feet. Human-sounding feet.

Ella groaned. She turned her head painfully. Nancy was crouching beside her, pulling at her headgear, lifting away the ear-flaps, then the mask with its prickly moustache.

'Lor, Ella, you gave me the frights when you came crashing down those stairs!' But Nancy was actually chuckling. 'I thought it was the real old Japanese Warrior come to life. You should've warned me you were going to hide inside it. What were you trying to do?'

'Get away from *that*!' Ella lifted one armour-clad arm and pointed upwards.

Miss Dearing came pattering down the stairs in her velvet slippers and long white nightgown. Her silvery hair was loose and fell almost to her waist. She snapped on the hallway light.

'Girls! Whatever's going on? I heard the strangest noises, so I got up to investigate. That's when I saw this *creature* come to life and tumble down the stairs. Quite terrifying! Please explain.'

'Did you see them?' asked Nancy, crouching over Ella and trying to loosen more bits of armour. 'Did you?'

'See who?' cried Miss Dearing. 'See what?'

'See the ghosts?' mumbled Ella.

'See the Shanto boys, that's who! They came stumbling past, dragging something out of Mr Duggan's museum room. A great big shield, it looked like. The battery on my torch went dead or I'd have seen them sooner and raised the alarm. When that warrior came flying towards them they shot right by me and disappeared down the cellar.'

'The Shanto boys!' Miss Dearing echoed loudly, and Ella feebly.

Nancy jumped to her feet. 'I knew it,' she said. 'Just needed proof.'

Ella scrambled out of the last bits armour herself, throwing the helmet away from her. The bristly moustache came off and lay on the floor like a giant centipede. 'Are we going after them?' Her voice came out more shakily than she expected. Her knees felt shaky too.

Nancy said urgently, 'Is your torch still working?'

Ella looked around. 'If I can find it,' she said.

'*No one* is going *anywhere*,' commanded Miss Dearing. 'Except to the Snuggery, where Nancy can light the fire and I will pour us all a fortifying tot of dandelion cordial. The Shanto boys—if it *were* they—can wait til tomorrow. I want an explanation from you two.'

Ella kicked at one of the warrior's feet with her own. This had not been such a brilliant idea after all.

56. LOW TIDE

NANCY'S JOURNAL

It was long after mid-night when Miss D. sent us to bed
& long after that before I fell asleep. Ella & me talked
for ages—wundering what would happen next. 'Those
Shanto boys must have got the fright of their lives,' was
the last thing Ella said. I replied 'For a change!' but she
was already snoring.

Next thing I knew was a voice shouting 'Donkeys out!'
I shot out of bed & into my clothes before my be-fuddled
mind worked out who it was (Peg) & what they were saying.
Ella was still rolled up like a caterpillar in eiderdown &
blankets. I shook her. Then I ran.

It was broad daylight already—that's how long we'd
overslept—& shaping up to be a sunny one. Which showed
the RUIN of the garden all too well.

- The donkey shelter—the one that <u>did</u> stand up to
  the storm—was in a heap squashing the Crokay-Lawn
  fence. All the donkeys were gone.
- The donkeys on the Bowling Green had crashed their
  fence too—maybe when they saw what their frends
  were up to.
- Hoof marks all over the wet grass & a <u>big gap</u> in a
  hedge which I'm sure the Storm never made.

I stared about wundering which way to go. That's when I saw Miss Dearing—heard her too—yelling 'Over here!!' She was quite the most Eccentric-looking I've ever seen her: wild white hair, check blanket & gumboots with nightdress underneath. Topped off with her purple turban (a bit sideways).

SAVE THE DONKEYS!

She was shooing Mr Oakapple before her—which is quite A TRIUMF to get him to do anything regarding donkeys! Peg was far off in the lead.

I should have known where we were headed—the beach. Tho I couldn't spot any donkeys at first. At Low Tide there's miles of sand to choose from & lots of little in-&-out bays between the rocks that you never see the rest of the time. I tried to keep to the dry sand & the rocks—the ones not covered in seaweed & slime—but even that was tricky as those are uneven & jagged & you are likely to BREAK AN ANKLE on them too.

Ella ran up just as the donkeys came into view. 'There's more of them than ever!' she said. They were right out under the cliffs on a bank of yellow sand. Much further out than last time.

That's when 2 things happened at once. Ella grabbed my arm & pointed at the water which was running in fast in tiny waves just like the frills on a posh party dress—& Peg gave a different sort of shout & vanished from view in the rocks.

57. FIRST AID

It was Ella who found Peg Shanto sprawled in a cleft in the rocks, one leg twisted beneath her and the other in a slick of wet sand that was rapidly filling with the incoming tide. Her face was screwed up in pain but she was still shouting instructions to the others. 'Keep 'em all together! Don't panic 'em!'

Ella stopped and crouched down. The twisted foot wasn't trapped—thank goodness—but when she touched the rubber boot Peg flinched and let out a squeak. Ella recalled the First Aid she had learned before going on one of her father's archaeological digs: keep the patient calm. Not that she'd ever had an actual patient before. She had never needed to tie a sling round a broken arm or twist a stick into a tourniquet to stop someone's life-blood from seeping away. Those both sounded very exciting. Peg Shanto with a twisted ankle, stuck on a beach that was quickly becoming the sea again, was quite a different prospect. And Peg was tall, much taller than Ella, and much heavier.

'Don't worry,' she said (wishing that someone could

230

say that to her). 'We'll have you back safe and sound in no time.'

'It's not me, it's the donkeys,' Peg groaned.

'Miss Dearing's dealing with them. And Nancy Parker. She's always first-rate in an emergency, I promise you.'

'The donkeys . . .' Peg repeated, and grimaced with pain.

Ella wedged herself under the taller girl's arm and somehow hauled her to her feet.

'We'll have to keep to the sand,' she said, even though that meant sloshing through the waves for the first part of their journey. Peg limped along gamely, gritting her teeth and drawing in sharp breaths, but never uttering another squeak. Ella thought she would collapse under the weight. Where Peg's arm was slung over her shoulders, she could feel the bruises she got last night from falling downstairs inside a suit of Japanese armour. But after all the dull weeks of school this was a glorious adventure! She'd far rather have freezing feet and a bruised back and be dragging an injured girl out of deadly danger than sit in class reciting Latin verbs.

Peg kept trying to look back, which didn't help Ella's precarious balance. 'Where are they? What's going on?' she asked.

'Never fear, they're doing splendidly,' said Ella, who didn't have a clue. 'Of course they are.'

Though of course they might all be under the waves by now, or trapped in one of those little coves with no way of escaping. She tried to keep these pictures out of her mind, and concentrate on thoughts of cloth torn into useful strips of bandage and where in heaven's name she might find a safety pin.

58. THE CAVE

NANCY'S JOURNAL

No idea how I got to them before Miss Dearing in her gum boots. Or Mr Oakapple (tho he <u>wasn't half so keen</u> on getting there as her & I can't really blame him.) With Peg out the way & Ella off helping her, it was just me & the donkeys on a tiny slip of beach. The sea was before us & cliffs above us. We gazed at each other—wundering what next? I can't swim. No idea if donkeys can.

Miss Dearing was calling out but she was stuck in another of those coves with the water sloshing over her night-gown & sharp slippery rocks between her & us. Mr Oakapple had bobbed out of sight.

Desperate, I twisted about looking for some way out—as if that could magic up a new bit of dry land—or stop the tide!! And thru the dazzle on the water I spotted A BOAT. It was hard to see for the sun shining so bright but I thoght I could make out 3 figures—1 rowing & 2 up the ends. The oars were moving fast.

As it got nearer I could see it was Spud & Ears Shanto (last spied dragging something down into the cellar!) in that row-boat of theirs—the one Mr Oak told me about. He's right. It's ever so small. I suppose they heard Peg shouting or spotted those donkeys stampeeding over the sands.

233

Spud was pulling on the oars so hard I thoght he would burst—and up the far end was none other than Alfred Lubbock!! But all the rowing in the world couldn't save a dozen donkeys on the smallest furthest-out bit of beach, hell-bent on sticking there & refusing to move.

Then Alfred took over the oars & the other 2 jumped out the boat! They splashed & thrashed around & then they were there—on my bit of beach—wet to the knees & above. They looked at me very foolish for a moment—cos I KNEW it was them last night up to no good—& they knew I knew. But they'd come to rescue me so I was willing to forget that for now. They might even carry me thru the waves to save me from getting wet!

As for the donkeys, I was ever so sorry but they'd got no one to blame but themselves for this awful pickle—with their habit of running away & their stubborn natures once they'd run.

But then Spud slopped right past me, water pouring from his britches & his boots. I thought he was going to grab a donkey or something (they might fit Little Jem in the row-boat at a pinch) but he went off into the rocks behind us—and DISAPPEARED. Then he came back & nodded to Ears. 'Right-o. Let's give it a go. Got to try— for Peg's sake.' Ears nodded back. 'Prove we're not such useless lummoxes as she thinks.'

It was the most I'd ever heard them say.

'Which one's the leader?' Spud said to me. He meant the donkeys. As if I knew! I saw Pancho give me a look—but it was a <u>worried look</u> like he'd bitten off more than he could chew—& I knew who I had to choose. Gilda. Pretty as a picture postcard but she always was the headstrong one. Spud said 'Take her into the cave & let's hope this lot follow.'

The CAVE!?

'No time to mess about!' Ears said when I just stood there. The water was already over my shoes & cold as Christmas. I'd lose the use of my toes if I stayed any longer. So I grabbed Gilda by the mane right above her shoulder and sort of pushed her forward. Maybe she was frightened too & just waiting for someone to tell her what to do cos—much to my supprise—she stepped forward. The other donkeys began nosing after her with Ears & Spud close behind them to stop anyone changing their mind.

Then we were at the mouth of The Cave. 'It's black as pitch in there!' I called out & Spud Shanto just growled back 'It's a cave. What d'you expect—silver shandeleers?'

One of them struck a match & I looked inside. I could see then that somehow we might not drown.

59. SURVEYING THE RUINS

Ella collapsed on to the sea-wall with a groan. Peg Shanto groaned too, but she managed a thin smile as well. 'That's our house, over there,' she nodded. 'Not far now.'

As Ella prepared to haul her upright for the last stretch, a rowing-boat bumped up into the shallows. Alfred Lubbock leaped out and helped Miss Dearing down. Mr Oakapple climbed out by himself.

'Where's Nancy?' Ella called to them. 'And the donkeys?'

She had a bad feeling in the pit of her stomach. What was it that Madame Arcana had said to Nancy? Something about *straying into dark places* and *dark forces pulling her down*. Was that the sea?

Miss Dearing shook her head and strode away up the beach, her wet clothes flapping. Mr Oakapple hopped along after her, looking extremely worried. Alfred pulled the boat up on to the shingle and stowed the oars safely. He said to Peg, 'Let's get you home. Is your Ma in?'

'No. It's her day for cleaning the church.'

Alfred took off his cap and rubbed his fair hair. 'Best bet is the Grange, then. We'll get you there somehow.' But he slumped down beside the other two on the sea wall, looking utterly drained. 'Blimey! I only came to take Miss Dearing for her driving lesson . . .'

'This do?' a voice behind them shouted. Ella turned to see Mr Oakapple pushing a big green wheelbarrow towards them. 'We'll give young Peg a ride like the May Queen 'erself.'

When they reached the Croquet Lawn, they found Miss Dearing wrapped in a grey wool dressing-gown, surveying the ruins. She picked a splintered signboard up off the grass. The words *Oxcoombe Grange Donkey Sanctuary* could still be made out, but there was a hoof–sized hole right through the middle of it.

'This was all a terrible mistake,' she said to herself. 'I should never have taken it on. Foolish creature that I am!'

She dragged the sign over to the gravel pathway and threw it down in disgust. 'Just look at your beautiful garden, too,' she said to Mr Oakapple. 'The work of years! I am so sorry.'

Mr Oakapple just rubbed his chin, as if he hardly knew what to make of such a turn in events.

Ella and Alfred helped Peg out of the wheelbarrow and sat her on the terrace steps.

'Have to cut that boot off,' Mr Oakapple told them.

'No sense in trying to pull it,' and Peg flinched at the very thought.

'There are some big scissors in the kitchen,' Miss Dearing began. 'Nancy would know where . . .'

Ella got up to go and find some. It was better to do something than just to sit around glooming. As she hurried along the path where the statues of old gods and goddesses stared out blankly from their ivy beds, she heard the strangest noise. A fierce, sharp creaking and cracking, as if a door was going to break or a window burst. She glanced up at the house but all was calm. The morning sun reflected off the windows, making them look blind.

But as she gazed upwards, dirt and dust and leaves sprang out at her, peppering her face and hair and wet clothes. The creaking crack turned into a roar and the world exploded.

60. MAD PANIC

NANCY'S JOURNAL

Spud Shanto led the way—using up a lot of matches before we got to the part of the cave where the ground grew dry. (I suppose the sea must never get that far.) There was a shelf in the rock there—with old oil lamps kept on it—& after that it got easier. If you can say trying to get a dozen SCARED DONKEYS down a dark narrow tunnel is easy!! Plus your heart is bumping right up in your throat & your legs feel like icy-cold jelly & your shoes are squelching with wet.

I was not keen on Donkeys before & I cannot say I am any keener now.

Smugglers! That's what the Shanto boys are—like their grandads & great grandads back over hundreds of years. It was a smuggler cave we went into—one you can only reach at low tide—& that led to a smuggler tunnel & I KNEW where it was going to go. I hoped they had a key to that big wide door—it was locked when I tried it. Cos me & 12 donkeys & 2 smugglers were going to be VERY STUCK otherwise.

Spud Shanto reached into another little nook where the key was stored & let us out. Which was a great releef. Until I realised—we were in a cellar with 12 donkeys milling round—and nowhere to go but steep curving steps. I may not know much about animals but I was pretty sure donkeys & stairs do not go together. The other tunnel ended in a <u>trapdoor</u>! What hope had we of getting those creatures out?!

'Now what?' said Spud. Ears just shrugged & looked as gormless as usual. It's clear that Peg has ALL THE BRAINS IN THE FAMILY.

'We can wait for the tide to go down and get them back that way' I said.

Spud frowned and Ears scratched his head. Spud said 'Be the middle of the night by then. Got to go careful with that cave. Tide won't be quite so low and them donkeys won't be happy.'

The donkeys weren't happy anyhow. They were nosing about in the archways & heaps of this & that like they'd always wanted to explore a cellar. But they kept nipping each other & pushing & setting back their ears so I knew it wouldn't be long before they were all in a MAD PANIC. It was a wonder that nobody had hurt themselves before now. Pancho had taken himself away into an arch that was stacked with broken chairs & cobwebby rocking-horses with missing legs & I could see he felt trapped & scared. I had to pull some of it out of his way.

To their credit the Shanto boys did give come & me

a hand & we worked faster then. That's when I saw the archway Pancho had chosen wasn't blocked up with bricks—it was blocked up with PLANKS OF WOOD. Spidery, mushroomy, rotten old wood with fingers of ivy pushing thru. If ivy could push one way maybe we could push the other. It wouldn't hurt to try.

Ears gave it a shove with his hands & when it creaked Spud gave it a good hard kick with his boot. (I didn't need to see what his footprint looked like. By now I knew.) A smell of fresh air blew in—& bits of daylight—& the donkeys got very CURIOUS. When you've got a dozen donkeys breathing down your necks you got to act fast. So we did.

Suddenly the cellar was full of light! The look on the faces of Ella—and Mr Oak—and poor Miss Dearing!! — as 12 adgitated donkeys skipped over the wreck of the ivy arch and kicked up their heels in the sun. With Pancho & Gilda leading the way they trotted down to the Crokay Lawn—& tho there were no fences left —they all stopped there & put their heads down to graze.

Dear Nancy,

Just a quick note to go with those mittens you asked for. I hope they turned out like you wanted. Your sketch was a touch hard to follow. I did not know what colours you had in mind so I used up scraps from my knitting basket—mustard & maroon with a bit of sky blue. Very jolly.

I hope you're keeping well & taking care to wrap up warm. They get nasty winter weather at the coast. Mind you don't get your feet wet & always get a good night's sleep.

Love from us all,

Grandma X

61. MISS DEARING'S IDEA

Professor Otter sat in the vast library of Oxcoombe Grange but his eyes did not stray to the bookshelves. They were fixed on Ella, who sat opposite.

'It was most unwise, Ella, to put yourselves in such danger. And in the course of your foolish actions you lied to Mrs Prebble.'

'Only on paper, Father,' Ella protested.

'That makes it *worse*.'

Ella said nothing. She kept her eyes down and a grave expression on her face. But she was bursting to *know*!

'At Miss Dearing's request,' her father went on, 'I have interviewed both Ears and Spud Shanto.' He pronounced these names as if just saying *Ears* and *Spud* gave him actual pain. 'I would prefer it if the matter was handed to the police, but Miss Dearing was adamant on that point. I have told her what I discovered. I suppose you want me to tell you?'

Ella's eyebrows nearly shot off her forehead. She nodded wildly. Was he honestly thinking of keeping the final result of all her and Nancy's hard work to himself?

'I believe you're familiar with the name of Vale?'

All Ella managed to say was, 'Yes, it's—,' before Professor Otter held up a hand to silence her.

'A certain Percival Vale, who lives just across the valley at Oriel House, was taking everything the Shantos could supply him with. He's a dealer of antiquities and curios with a shop in London—far enough away to think that none of it would be recognized.'

'Did he pay them?' Ella managed to get in.

'Of course he did, but only a fraction of what he must have made when he sold the items on. The Shantos hadn't a clue about their worth. Thought they were quaint old rubbish, really. But someone was willing to pay, so . . . Those young men weren't old enough to fight in the War, their pride was hurt, and they wanted to revive the tradition of their grandfathers and great-grandfathers.'

'Smuggling!'

'A sort of smuggling.'

Like my sort-of plan, Ella thought. 'He must be Mrs Vale's husband and Juniper's father,' she said. 'What a rotten crooked lot. They need to be brought to justice. *All* of them.'

Professor Otter looked thoughtful. 'Miss Dearing has an idea . . .' he said.

There was a knock at the door.

'She's not nearly as silly and flustered as she pretends,' the professor added in a low voice.

Then Nancy, in a clean white apron and borrowed shoes, came in with a tray of tea.

62. A BLIND EYE

NANCY'S JOURNAL

After that last adventure Miss Dearing will not hear a word against the Shanto boys. Even wants to help them find proper jobs!

I tried to ask Peg—in a kindly way—if she knew all along what Spud & Ears were up to. But she all she did was bite her lip & shake her head. I think that means they were ALWAYS UP TO SOMETHING. But they _are_ her brothers. And they _did_ rescue the donkeys. And Peg is not one for words.

Miss Dearing says the family has been down on their luck for years—ever since Mr Shanto drownded. It was kindness to let them take coal & jam & what-not from her godfather's left-overs. Yes, she had turned a blind eye to it. What good Christian wouldn't? She does not CARE A FIG for Dominic Duggan's collection of masks & heads & horrors—& if someone wants to cart them away she's happy.

(Of course she didn't mean cart them away on the sly so some no-good trickster could Make a Mint from them.)

She says she only cares for God's creatures & that was why she is giving up on Oxcoombe Grange and going home to Apple Cottage which being small & cosy suits her much better. A farmer is renting her some big fields at the back—with hedges they call Stock-Proof (nothing can get out) —and the donkeys will live there. Well away from THE LURE OF THE SEASIDE. That's what Miss D. calls it. Seems that you can free a donkey from trudging along the beach all day giving children rides—but you can't free a donkey from dreaming of sand & sea.

Peg is going with the donkeys too—soon as her Sprained Ankle is better. Miss Dearing says she can sleep in the spare bedroom. So she's got no need of a Housekeeper & no room for one. But she promised she will write me the best ~~cart~~ caracter reference for my next place that any servant ever had. 'They will probbly let you look after the King when they read it!' she said. (Must say I don't want to work for the King. I wish she would write that I was Excellent at Solving Mysteries.)

I wasn't even a very good Housekeeper. Despite Lady Pouncey's Wise Advice I got just about EVERYTHING wrong. Tho I did learn how to make a nice Vedgetarian pie.

So I've been busy this past week packing everything up. But now I'm sitting with my feet up on the Excelsior for the last time & waiting for Alfred to drive me to the station. I turned down the chance of a ride in the donkey cart. Besides it is raining again.

I passed those gloves Gran sent on to Ella cos she is

always losing hers. When she saw the colours she made an odd sort of noise but she took them anyway.

Ella got an A+ in English for writing a story about our latest adventures. I said I hope you didn't tell the teacher to look in the newspaper this time—but she says she changed all the names & claimed it was made up. Besides—they never put the whole story in the paper.

But I did save a few ITEMS OF INTEREST out of recent copies of the 'Seabourne Herald' & shall stick them in here anyway.

GIFT TO MUSEUM

A most generous gift has been made to Seabourne Museum by Miss E. M. Dearing, in memory of her godfather, the late Mr Dominic Duggan of Oxcoombe Grange. Mr Duggan's entire collection of foreign artefacts, including many rare and valuable items such as ancient carved figures and antique armour, will be on display at the Museum by next summer.

In addition, Mr Percival Vale of Oriel House, near Oxcoombe, will be donating a number of items in keeping with

Mr Duggan's collection. Mr Vale has long been a keen collector of foreign works of art but has decided, along with Mrs Vale, to give his time and attention to local good causes. On hearing of Miss Dearing's generous actions, he has joined her in making his own collection available to the public.

Miss Dearing is kindly endowing funds to refurbish the Museum entirely so that the collection may be seen at its best. While these works are carried out the Museum will be closed for six months. The Public Library will remain open during this time. The Reference Library will unfortunately be closed.

FRAUD FLEES EXPOSURE

It is reported that the Medium and Psychic going under the name of 'Madame Arcana' left Seabourne in a hurry last week, amid rumours of fraud. It is not known where the so-called medium has fled to, although it is believed that she usually resides in London. Further engagements in Brighton have been cancelled. The bill for use of a room in Seabourne's Grand Hotel, where 'Madame Arcana' held private audiences, remains unpaid.

SCHOOL NEWS

Hockey

The previously undefeated 1st XI from Seabourne Girls' Grammar Lower School were beaten by the team from Warne Court with a score of 25–0. This surprising result may be due to the absence of Seabourne's captain, Miss Juniper Vale. Miss Vale has taken an extended leave of absence due to sudden ill health and is said to be travelling to sunnier climes with her mother.

YOUNG WOMEN'S TRAINING COLLEGE TO OPEN

A Residential Training College to prepare young women for employment in the horticultural trades will be opening shortly. Miss Winifred Parry has announced that she will be heading the college, which will be housed in Oxcoombe Grange, known for its formal gardens dating from the early 1800s.

Miss Parry expects there to be places for 20 young women in the new year, with plans for further expansion. 'The horticultural trades should not be solely for men,' Miss Parry commented. 'Women have already proved their worth as accomplished gardeners. Our new college is a very valuable opportunity for the practical education of young women.'

Mr Joshua Oakapple, Head Gardener, will continue to oversee the gardens.

Oxcoombe Grange was formerly a private house, and, most recently, a donkey sanctuary.

63. THE GREY LADY

NANCY'S JOURNAL

Scribbling this on the train home.

Just had to put down what Alfred said on the way to the station. He drives that motor car much more smooth & steady than Miss Dearing. (She's agreed to have 1 or 2 more lessons before she takes it out again!)

Alfred was his same carefree chatty self. 'Back to the big city eh? What did you think of Oxcoombe then?' he asked. I told him just what I told his Ma—I may be have been somewhat <u>less polite</u> this time as I won't ever be there again. But I said that I got to like Mr Oak and Peg—and even the donkeys a bit. Can't say I'm sad to see the back of that old house. Too big. Too cold & drafty. Too much dust.

'That all?' he said. We stopped by the station & he got my suitcase out the back. 'I never said before—didn't want to put the wind up—but anyhow you're a Down-to-Earth girl.'

What? I wanted to know. WHAT?

'Old Violet Cummings told me there's a grey lady that walks about upstairs. Miss Cummings used to work at the Grange DONKEYS YEARS ago.' He found that last bit <u>very funny</u>. Almost split his sides.

The Seabourne train was steaming in so I dashed on

to the platform. Alfred shouted after me: 'Ghost of an olden-times housekeeper, Miss Cummings says. All nonsense of course. Nobody else ever saw her.'

And that's the last I saw of Alfred—his big grin as the train pulled away.

ABOUT THE AUTHOR

JULIA LEE

Julia Lee has been making up stories for as long as she can remember. She wrote her first book aged 5, mainly so that she could do all the illustrations with a brand-new 4-colour pen, and her mum stitched the pages together on her sewing machine. As a child she was ill quite a bit, which meant she spent lots of time lying in bed and reading (bliss!).

Julia grew up in London, but moved to the seaside to study English at university, and has stayed there ever since. Her career has been a series of accidents, discovering lots of jobs she didn't want to do, because secretly she always wanted to be a writer.

Julia is married, has two sons, and lives in Sussex.

ALSO BY JULIA LEE

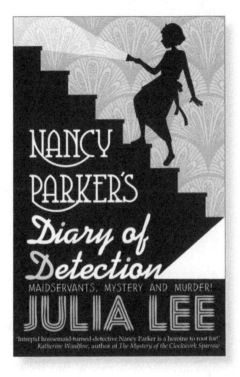

When Nancy Parker gets her first position as a housemaid to Mrs Bryce, it's not exactly her dream job—she'd rather be out solving mysteries. But she soon discovers there are plenty of suspicious occurrences going on beneath her very nose . . . Time for Nancy to set to work not just with her mop but also with her Theory of Detection!

ISBN: 978-0-19-273938-4

A plucky orphan, a dark family secret,
and a thrilling race against time . . .

Clemency is utterly penniless and entirely alone, until
she's taken in by the marvellous Marvels—a madcap
family completely unlike her own. But it's a surprise
to them all when she's mysteriously bundled from the
house by the frightening Miss Clawe.

Concerned about Clemency's fate, the Marvels
set out to find her. Enlisting the help of some
not-quite-genuine Red Indians, it's a calamitous race
across the country. But Clemency's misadventures are
more dire than her rescuers suspect . . . will they
reach her in time?

ISBN: 978-0-19-273367-2

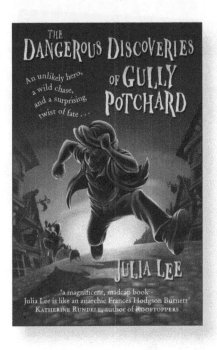

An unlikely hero, a wild chase, and a
surprising twist of fate . . .

'a magnificent, madcap book—Julia Lee is like an
anarchic Frances Hodgson Burnett'
Katherine Rundell, author of *Rooftoppers*

Gully Potchard never meant to cause any trouble. He's
just an ordinary sort of boy . . . at least that's what he
thinks. But when an old acquaintance comes knocking,
mischief and skulduggery follow—and soon Gully
discovers that he has an extraordinary skill which
might just make him an unlikely hero after all . . .

ISBN: 978-01-9-273369-6

Ready for more great stories? Try one of these...

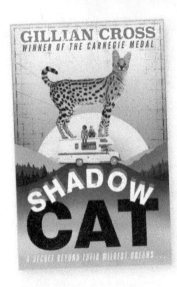

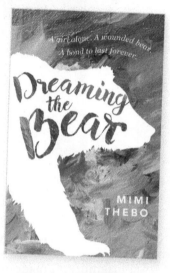